Praise for
On the Way to Red Square

"On the Way to Red Square exceeds the boundaries it has created for itself: between the private and the political, the everyday and the theatrical, love and alienation, informers and their victims, life and death, joy and sadness, Russians and foreigners, 'us' versus 'them.' The ineffable language of pain and inquisitive openness and the resulting vision of the stern Soviet Moscow is hauntingly revealing, at the same time the distant and the close glance that Victor Shklovsky aptly defines."

-Olga Meerson, Professor of Russian, Georgetown University.

"Julieta Rodrigues has neatly captured the gray, gritty, every-day essence of life in the Soviet Union that I saw in the early 1980's. From the snowy and dismal streets to the bath-houses and garish hotels, she has preserved lost fragments of communist Moscow in her amber stories. Our brief encounters with her characters reveal a system dreadfully impersonal and insensitive, one that made even the simplest aspects of life burdensome and forced people to be suspicious where suspicion would not normally be warranted. Perhaps the greatest strength of her work, however, is that by the end of the book it is the characters and their emotions, not the model communist city, which leave the most lasting impression."

-Jon Purnell, Tashkent, Uzbekistan.

"In a book as teaming with characters as a 19th-century Russian novel, but entirely modern in its concerns, we accompany Laura, narrator and protagonist, through gripping and candid stories: the angry young man in 'Caged,' living in a cramped collective where people must line up to use the toilet; the disappointed, power-abusing official, Lyudmila, in 'Glass Silhouettes,' obsessed with her collection of miniatures; the charming stranger in 'The Puppetmaster,' whose invitation Laura must refuse for fear he is a KGB agent; the belligerent woman in 'Last Chance,' whose envy gets Laura into trouble at the public baths; and, in the last story, 'New Year's Eve at the Praga,' an enigmatic blonde dancing alone, as intriguing and ambiguous to the little band of Americans as is Moscow itself.

Julieta Rodrigues reminds me of Chekhov."

-Robbie Murphy, *Best American Short Stories* (under the name of Roberta Gupta).

Professor Julieta Almeida Rodrigues has taught courses in sociology, politics, creative writing, literature and culture at the University of Lisbon and Georgetown University. She has published in the field of sociology and has been a speaker in various international fora. The first story of this collection was published in the literary journal *Gávea-Brown* (2001-2002). With this collection, Professor Rodrigues expands her writings into the field of literature.

On the Way to Red Square

On the Way to Red Square

Stories
by Julieta Almeida Rodrigues

SCARITH An imprint of New Academia Publishing, LLC
Washington, DC

Printed in the United States of America
Library of Congress Control Number: 2005909637
ISBN 0-9767042-7-7 paperback (alk. paper)

 An imprint of New Academia Publishing, LLC
P.O. Box 27420, Washington, DC, 20038-7420
www.newacademia.com - info@newacademia.com

To Mark,
for adventures in fiction.
To Julian,
for my dreams
at the time.

Contents

Foreword   *xi*

On the Way to Red Square   1
Caged   11
Flames for a Revolution   23
Glass Silhouettes   33
Border Crossing   45
Lost Chance   55
On the Trail of Tolstoy   67
The Puppetmaster   81
At the Embassy's Dacha   93
Farewell, Dear Friend and Comrade   103
At the Kosmos Hotel   113
Crescendo   125
When Alliluyeva Returned   137
At the Levins'   153
New Year's Eve at the Praga   163

Foreword

This book is based on my experiences in Moscow in 1983-86 as the wife of a young American diplomat. The conditions under which my husband and I lived were most intriguing and, as a sociologist, I became a keen observer and note-taker during our stay.

To build the stories, I jotted down every single detail that caught my eye. In this sense, my stories have an autobiographical basis. The bay window in Oleg's apartment was there, and his mother loved it with a passion; I did visit the local cemetery with a dear friend when we spent a few days at the embassy dacha; the sensuous blonde was, indeed, at the New Year's Eve party at the Praga Hotel. The man immolating himself in Red Square, Andropov's funeral, and Svetlana Alliluyeva returning to the Soviet Union, were actual events that occurred while we lived in Moscow. Those were the times.

As Don DeLillo puts it:

> I think fiction comes from everything you've ever done, and said, and dreamed, and imagined. It comes from everything you've read and haven't read. It comes from all the things that are in the air…the work itself…it's much too intimate, much too private, to come from anywhere but deep within the writer himself.
>
> (Conversations with Don DeLillo, 2005).

I believe in this. Had I not been to Moscow, I would not have written this collection of stories. Of the characters described, only the public figures actually existed, as did the times in which they lived; the stories themselves are the creation of a fictional imagination.

I would like to thank a long list of friends and colleagues who helped me on my way. They are a part of me and, therefore, are a part of these stories as well. They helped me with computer skills, commented on the manuscript, gave me discerning opinions, and polished my English. I would like to mention: Dana Brentt, Abbey Mattes, Christine Svitlana Otsver, David L. Hoof, Maryanne Ozernoy, Marija K. Del Bono, Joseph and Leslie Teixeira, Valerie Hanlon, Cara Goodman, Beth Huse, Teresa Greenwald, Cynthia Roderick, Edward Steinberg, the late Natasha Deakin, Lavinia Cavalletti, José Sasportes and Ana Mantero. Special thanks go to Professor Clea Rameh, who kindly opened the doors of the Spanish and Portuguese Department, Georgetown University, where I was an Adjunct Professor in Portuguese in 2001, 2002 and 2004; Professor Jeffrey Anderson, Director, BMW Center for German and European Studies, Georgetown University, where I was an Adjunct Professor in the Spring of 2004, thanks to the generous support of the Luso-American Foundation; Professor Amélia Hutchinson, for her insightful comments; Martha S. Daza, for her understanding of human nature; Ruth Purnell for editing the first edition, and Gail Spilsbury for editing the second, revised edition. Last but not least, I feel fortunate that Professor Anna Lawton appreciated my stories and offered to publish them.

1983-1986

On the Way to Red Square

A Portuguese in Moscow, I woke up that Sunday morning to find that Keith was not in bed with me. When I opened the curtains in the nearby window, slowly measuring my gestures, a feeling of impending doom spread over my body. I was from a sunny country, to catch a glimpse of the weather was a vital need. My fear of a cold, bitter winter was instinctive that Sunday in late October. After all, Moscow was as far north as I had ever lived.

I had reason for concern. In the last few days the temperature had fallen well below freezing, and a few orphan snowflakes had swirled here and there. But the true sign of the approaching winter had been a steady wind, a glacial blast that froze the very marrow of my bones. On Friday evening, the weather forecast had predicted heavy snow for the following days. As I peered out my bedroom window, I felt alone, forsaken.

Crows flapped restlessly in the square below making shrill, awful noises. When the square was empty—as it always was on weekends—the crows assembled there. I had no sympathy for those birds: black, repulsive, unfriendly. They filled the square in clusters of five or six, gathered mostly towards the left corner near the sidewalk. Only God knew why they chose that spot; my guess was that it provided shelter from the inclement weather.

When the birds were not there, the square was almost

pleasing. I enjoyed the quaint, old-fashioned aura of the faded cream and yellow facades on the other side of the street. The few, solitary trees were stripped naked, their frail limbs reaching for the sky. That early in the season, the narrow pedestrian paths leading to the *gastronom* on the ground floor were still open. Customers continued to stop and buy provisions at the store since various items, such as dried foods, remained available.

I made my way to our small kitchen to prepare coffee, avoiding Keith, who was listening to music through his earphones in the living room. To reach the kitchen I had to cross the far end of the room. I did not greet Keith, and he might not have seen me. The large, dark-green lampshade topping the brass lamp near his armchair blocked me from his view. Besides, he had not turned in my direction.

The kitchen was scarcely more than a corridor and, as soon as I came in, I shied away from the window that stood opposite the door. I needed time to get used to the wire fence that enclosed the courtyard on that side of the building. The Soviets said the fence was there to protect us, the foreigners. But protect us from what?

Keith and I had arrived only a few months before, and I still had not fully adjusted to my new environment. Keith, an American, had been assigned to the American Embassy, his first diplomatic post. Moscow, capital of the USSR, Union of Soviet Socialist Republics, had become, thus, our first home as recent newlyweds. Friends had warned me of the difficulties that lay ahead, but somehow, I had been oblivious to them. Now the fence reminded me, ominously, of a concentration camp. By a stroke of luck, I could not see the booth of the *militsioner*, the uniformed police officer who stood day and night by the entrance to the building's parking lot.

Quickly, however, I had become fond of our kitchen. The mixture of light brown tiles and matching cupboards had appealed to me from the day we arrived. The stove was almost new, the refrigerator was in the right place, and it was easy to move around; easy, that is, if only one of us was there.

I made my coffee and sat on a small bench to drink it. Its sensuous smell and the warm cup in my hands filled my heart. Seated, I found comfort that the wire fence was not visible anymore. I could see only the low building across the way, where the three perpetually shaded windows proved that Keith and I were not unaccompanied. Watching eyes inspected us, how many we did not know.

As I stared out the window, snow started to fall. First slowly, but soon larger and larger flakes appeared before my eyes. It was magical, cotton balls were floating down from the sky, a manna from the gods. Standing up, I realized that the courtyard's ground was turning, little by little, into a mantle of thick, white, powdered sugar. The snow seemed a blessing intended for me personally, and my mood, miraculously, started to improve. I stood still for long minutes, noticing, in awe, how my coffee tasted even better.

I thought a walk in the snow might be a good idea, so I rushed to the living room and shouted over the earphones, "Keith! Good morning! Do you want to go for a walk? Look, it's snowing!"

Removing the earphones uneasily, Keith replied, "Good morning, Laura. What did you say?"

"It's snowing," I repeated excitedly, pointing at the window. "It's so beautiful! The first winter snow might be the best moment for the next six months." And, again, "Do you want to go for a walk?"

"I want to finish this piece of music. We can go afterwards."

"Why can't you finish it later?"

"I want to finish it now."

"But we don't know how long the snow will last." I

paused for a second, but then persisted, trying to sound casual, "What're you listening to?"

"It's Mahler."

"Again? Which piece?"

"It's the 'Songs on the Death of Children' in *Kindertotenlieder*."

"I wish you'd stop listening to those songs, they're so sad," I said, coming closer to him.

Barely looking at me, Keith answered apologetically, "I like them, you know that."

Before, Keith had loved the snow, truly enjoyed it. At the moment, however, not even the virgin white carpet spread outside could seduce him. Nothing could, for that matter. Once more, I wondered about the dispirited quality of the songs he kept listening to. They seemed almost subversive under our present circumstances. A coincidence was unlikely: could the songs be a factor in sustaining Keith's emotional freeze?

I looked at my husband intently but, unable to reply, I thought it best to go into the bedroom to dress. The task required effort, it might take as long as twenty minutes to prepare for the first winter snow. The embassy had cautioned us that certain procedures needed to be followed. Rule number one, dress warmly, seemed simple enough. Rule number two, dress in layers—several thin sweaters rather than one or two heavy ones—seemed reasonable and better for body flexibility. Rule number three, make sure the extremities—toes, fingers, ears—are warm at all times, was not exactly news to me. It reminded me of my Washington neighbor, dear old Dr. Altschuler, and how his dream of becoming a surgeon had died one day in the Moscow of his youth, together with his frozen fingers. Rule number four was the best of all—never, ever, face the Russian winter without a hat covering your head!

As I put on one layer after another, I recalled the instructions carefully. First came a bra and pantyhose. Then came thermal underwear, top and bottoms, as thin as a sheet of paper. Next was a light turtleneck sweater, long sleeved, plus two or three thicker ones. Lastly, I needed woolen pants, woolen socks, and leg warmers.

My sheepskin coat hung in the closet, and next to it were my woolen scarf and gloves. The coat came down to my ankles and had gorgeous bone buttons. When I put it on, somehow it always felt like the embrace of an old friend. My knee-high boots were fur-lined as well. Near them stood the amusing detail—my *shapka*.

I had bought the elegant fur hat in Helsinki on our way to Moscow. Dark brown, it had a layer of sable around the rim which covered my ears snugly. A stylish fur ball on an embroidered cord hung from the top. Looking into the mirror that first snowy day, I placed the ball on the left side, between my eye and ear. The hat felt so good, I could not help smiling.

Surprisingly, Keith was ready to go by the time I finished dressing. "You didn't want to wait for me but, in the end, I was ready first," he said.

"How did you do that? You're so cunning, I can't believe it."

"You think so?"

"Yes, I do. First you sat listening to that lugubrious music. Then you got ready, it seemed, while I was adjusting my hat. I didn't even hear you."

"Is that my fault?"

"No, but it's as if you're blaming me for taking time to wear the *shapka* the way I want it. I needed the perfect angle."

"Did I question you?"

"No, you didn't. But you could have complimented me."

"About what?"

"My *shapka*, the way I'm wearing it, how I look."

"This conversation is going nowhere. Why don't we just stop talking and get out?"

Happy in my *shapka*, compliments or not, I swung the fur ball with my hand as I looked up at Keith. He looked back at me momentarily. His eyes sparkled but remained, somehow, cold. He then gestured for me to go ahead of him and, after passing through the apartment's front door, we exited the building together.

As usual, the *militsioner* stood by the entrance to the parking lot near a placard with Cyrillic characters that indicated strangers were forbidden from entering the diplomatic compound. I tried to ignore the irritating sight. The policeman saluted us as we passed, a customary greeting I still had not got used to.

Snow continued to fall, now heavier than before. The flakes were bright, thick, and close to each other. Our boots were already covered in white and we had barely left the building. We walked north in Bolshaya Ordynka, our street, heading towards Red Square. Our boots made a crunching noise as we went along—regular, predictable, consistent. We needed to watch carefully where we stepped, otherwise we might lose our balance and fall. Once in a while, Keith leaned forward to help me along the barely visible sidewalk.

We pushed ahead as usual: silently, without physical contact, arms next to the body. The street was deserted, we seemed to be the first ones to walk it that day. Why would Russians venture out on a Sunday morning with a blizzard underway?

In order to admire our neighborhood we proceeded slowly and were soon immersed in a land of white enchantment. The two- and three-story high stucco buildings evoked the feeling that we were in nineteenth-century Moscow. Nobles and merchants had lived in the district for centuries, and the area retained an affluent ambience. This came as no surprise to us: after all, we were a mere ten-minute walk from the Kremlin, the heart of Moscow, where the Soviet oligarchy currently ruled.

We continued mushing along like dogs pulling a sled, shoulders hunched forward, eyes shuddering with frost. Not only our boots but also our faces, scarves, gloves, and hats were covered with snow by now. Occasionally, Keith reached for his glasses using one of his gloves as a windshield wiper. The thin, bare trees along the street looked as if they had been spray-painted with milk. The air was an exquisite elixir.

Perilous as it was, I compulsively looked up in search of a baby on one of the balconies. I had heard that Russians considered the winter especially invigorating, and the tradition of swaddling babies and bringing them outside for strength was still in practice. I would not be able to see a tiny face, but an old-fashioned pram would probably be visible.

Further down the street, close to the Church of the Virgin of All Sorrows, a boy, maybe seven, gazed out the window from his ground-floor apartment. The window's white trim framed his face like a painting. The boy was still wearing his pajamas, one hand pressing against the glass, fingers spread out. As we approached the church, he watched us closely; then he turned his attention to several others who rushed by to attend the Sunday service.

I turned to Keith softly, "Did you see that kid? He looked like a Rembrandt painting. Pity the window was so grubby!"

"Yes, I noticed him too. Such a wondrous gaze."

"He's a million years away from Mahler's dead children."

"Mmm, you're right, Laura."

"Keith, we should try for another baby soon. I'm sure

everything will be okay this time."

"I hope so."

I wanted to enter the church to participate in the Russian Orthodox ritual—the All Sorrows Church had a most captivating name. Although the Soviet Union was officially atheistic, lots of people were going in. Always the diplomat, Keith escorted me inside but remained near the entrance. I, on the other hand, made my way to the altar. It was fascinating to observe that the notion of personal space was totally absent; everybody was packed tightly, body touching body. Along the walls, small altars reached by steps honored various Orthodox saints. Colored oil lamps illuminated icons blackened by candle soot and age, their lively warmth in sharp contrast to the numbing cold outside.

At the altar, the Orthodox priest shook an oblong silver chest to spread incense, and its smell send a soothing fragrance throughout the church. The priest's gold and black embroidered robe and mitre, together with his long white beard, were imposing. I knelt, asking God to help Keith and me conceive again soon. A choir upstairs sang with radiance and, without hesitation, I thought of it as entirely female. And, yes, those voices sounded like angels.

Soon outside again, we pressed on in the direction of Red Square as many latecomers continued to bustle past us to enter the church. A young couple with their child hurried up the church steps, the mother trying to help her son keep his balance. Probably afraid the little one might fall and hurt himself, the woman held him by his scarf; as both wore clumsy fur gloves, there was no way to hold hands. The toddler held his arms out straight, a small crucified Christ.

The story of Dr. Altschuler's frozen fingers came back to mind. One day, as a medical student rushing to attend an early class, he had forgotten his gloves at home. It was deadly cold, the trolley was full, and he had had to cling to the outdoor rail for support. When he got to his stop, his right hand would not obey—the fingers were stuck to the rail. With warm water people helped him to pry his fingers loose, but his hand was never the same. That was the day his cherished dream collapsed.

Still walking, I turned to Keith, "I just remembered Dr. Altschuler's fingers, how he froze them on the trolley rail."

"That's such a painful story."

"I'm so sorry he's dead and we can't tell him where we are."

"The last time we saw him, I had the impression he was hanging on to life just to see who you married."

"He would have been so sorry to hear about my miscarriage."

"If you had taken better care of yourself..."

"Please don't start that again," I interrupted Keith abruptly. "The doctor said that the baby died inside of me."

"I know, but I can't help thinking that things could have turned out differently."

"Yes, perhaps they could have, but they didn't. That's life. I've dealt with this issue long enough, I need to move on."

"The boy in the window made me think about it again. We could have been parents by now."

"I'm sure we will be soon," I said reassuringly. "I said a prayer when we went into the church."

"You did? I'm glad."

Soon we reached the Moscow River Bridge at the end of Bolshaya Ordynka, I was eager to see the Kremlin by the embankment. And there it stood against the gray sky, ancient in its majesty. As in a fairy tale, sheets of snow shifted back and forth across its multi-shaped roofs. Closer to us, almost opposite the bridge, stood St. Basil's—dignified, mythical.

Stopping by the bridge, we stamped our feet on the ground to keep warm, our arms wrapped around our own bodies, not each other's. The enjoyment of the view helped us replenish our energy. We had been out in the storm for quite a while.

Ready to turn around for home, my eyes watery and my nose frozen, I looked at Keith's face. A few snowflakes clung to his mustache. I smiled at him and reaching out, hoping not to be rebuked, I brushed the snow from his whiskers with my glove.

Keith smiled back. His eyes were also watery and cold, but this time the physical world had taken over his body, not some chilly reflection from within. "How about going back home?" I asked.

"Let's do that," he answered.

"I can warm up some soup. We can also have the *blini* that I made yesterday with sour cream and black caviar. Would you like that?" I asked, craving the idea of a feast of Russian pancakes.

"I would love it, Laura," he replied, livelier than before.

"That boy in the window did more for you than words can describe, am I right?" I asked, inquisitive. "Or was it the walk, or even my prayer in the church?"

"I just feel peaceful, if only for a moment. That's all," Keith said. As he spoke, he took my hand and, shaking the snowflakes from my glove, placed it inside his pocket.

Caged

A few months after Keith and I settled in Bolshaya Ordynka Street, Jessica, an American student of Russian literature at MGU, the Moscow State University, asked me to go with her to visit her friend, Oleg. Pleasantly surprised at the opportunity to visit a Soviet home, I agreed. Jessica told me that she had met Oleg at a lecture. He was a researcher at a sociological institute and lived in a communal apartment near the Bolshoi Theater, away from his wife and child.

When Jessica confided that Oleg might be cracking under stress, I thought it better not to ask for details. I was afraid that she might withdraw the invitation. However, my curiosity in meeting Oleg only increased. Since I was feeling somewhat isolated both in my marriage and in the fenced compound, the invitation was like a call to freedom.

If American diplomats so desired, they could spend an entire assignment without making contact with the average Soviet. Jessica, however, had lived in Moscow for several months already, and as she was not part of the diplomatic community, was known to have many Russian acquaintances. She was the friend of a friend at the American Embassy and had been to our house for dinner. Without mentioning Oleg's address, I warned Keith of what we were up to. Everything seemed in order.

The invitation to visit Oleg was for lunch at three o'clock in the afternoon. Jessica had told me that Oleg wanted a late lunch so that he could have the communal kitchen mostly to himself. She had made the arrangements face-to-face, for using the telephone might put Oleg or his family in danger. Jessica tested my Russian to make sure that I could handle the conversation.

We met at Prospekt Marx Metro Station near a stand where *pirozhki* were being sold. The greasy smell of the well-known meat pies filled the air. As soon as we exchanged greetings, Jessica told me to walk fast. As we dashed down the street, she looked back to make sure we were not being tailed. On a nearby wall, a huge red banner screamed, "Transform Moscow into the Model Communist City."

I perspired profusely as we climbed the winding stairs to Oleg's eighth floor. By the time we reached an imposing, dark wood door ravaged by time, I was struggling to catch my breath. Jessica had not wanted to use the elevator—a tenant riding up with us might ask questions. Silently, we reached a landing decorated with tiny gray, white, and brown tiles. At last, Jessica pointed to a scuffed door armored with a long bank of locks.

Oleg opened the door as soon as Jessica tapped. Most probably he had been standing behind it, waiting for us. Without a word, he bowed his head and rushed us through a dark, narrow corridor. People were walking back and forth between apartments and communal areas. A dim ceiling light showed the way. Oleg opened another door with a key, and we entered a stuffy, windowless room. In the middle of that room he pushed aside a curtain suspended by a rope. We entered yet another room.

The vibrant winter sun shone through an old-fashioned bay window. The window dominated the entire tiny space, its panes decorated with antique stained glass. An old lady sat near a table, looking out. I paused to admire the woodwork encircling the windowpanes and the rooftops visible across the street in the afternoon light.

Removing her jacket, Jessica introduced me to Oleg. He looked over thirty-five, undernourished and serious, and wore dingy blue jeans with a heavy sweater that had once been off-white.

"And this is Oleg's mother, Marina Nikolaevna," said Jessica, pointing to the lady by the window.

I stepped over to greet her. She was small and thin, with powerful, piercing, dark eyes. She turned to me with a sharp smile on her lips. Her eyes, however, contradicted the smile. It was as if the eyes were probing me, the smile just a cover up.

"Pleased to meet you, too," I said, thinking she must be fascinated by foreigners.

The room was run down, cluttered. The sunshine highlighted the dust that covered everything. The wood floors had not been polished in decades. Used books filled a broken bookshelf and overflowed into small piles everywhere. To move, we had to squeeze between miniature towers of oddly shaped volumes. Oleg's interests spanned sociology, literature, international affairs, and foreign languages.

The only orderly place in the room was the table, already set with the *zakuski*, the tasty hors-d'oeuvres of the Russian cuisine. It was covered by an immaculate white tablecloth, obviously brand new for the occasion. Oleg invited Jessica and me to seat down while Marina Nikolaevna merely turned her chair around. The room was so small that I was at one end of the table squirming for space; a couch that doubled up as a bed pressed against my right leg.

Still standing, Oleg urged his two guests to taste the dainty "little bites." They smelled divine. He addressed us, "Come on, eat, this is why the food is here," he said nervously. "Try the black bread with the beet salad, it's really good." He poured indiscriminately either vodka or *Tsinandali*, a Georgian white wine, into our glasses.

Marina Nikolaevna did not need prompting to eat. She

helped herself to large portions, filling her plate, eating quickly, then filling the plate again. Oleg glanced at her a couple of times, unable to dissuade her with his eyes. Finally he scolded her, "You have to slow down. I cooked for my friends, not for you."

"Why should I?" she replied. "It's not every day that you prepare good food."

To change the subject, Jessica insisted that Oleg sit down, which he did. Turning to me, he said anxiously, "Laura, I'm so sorry that my wife, Yelena, couldn't come for lunch. Jessica is so fond of her. She lives in Yugo-Zapadnaya now, far out, and has to take our son, Kolya, to kindergarten every morning. Then she takes the metro to her office on Prospekt Kalinin. She is quite worn out these days."

"Doesn't she like this apartment?"

"No, it's not that. We can't live together now. We suffer, but there is nothing we can do."

"How sad."

"Before we got married, Yelena lived with her mother and I lived with mine." Oleg ate as he talked and seemed to find it increasingly difficult to swallow his food. "When we married, we asked our mothers to live together in one apartment so that we could have the other. Yelena and I moved into this place, it's closer to her work."

"It goes without saying that Marina Nikolaevna hated to part with her bay window," Jessica said.

Food in her mouth, Marina Nikolaevna answered, "You're right, Jessica, this window is my pride and joy."

"You didn't care for our marriage. If you had, you would have stayed there," Oleg said angrily.

She did not answer and continued to eat instead.

Oleg excused himself and got up. He pushed the curtain to one side and opened the apartment door again. We heard his steps in the narrow corridor. Minutes later he returned carrying the main course: roasted chicken, mushrooms cooked in butter, and yet another assortment of different kinds of sliced white and black bread. As he sat, he insisted again that Jessica and I eat more.

"As I was saying, our mothers didn't get along well," Oleg continued. "My mother hated the new neighborhood. The two women hated each other. They fought all the time."

"What a pity!" I said.

"No, it's not a pity," Marina Nikolaevna said looking me straight in the eyes. "I belong in this apartment, I've lived here all my life."

"You see how she is." Oleg pointed his fork to his mother while he talked to me. "I don't have to explain anything." Grim, he went on, "Half-jokingly Yelena and I thought of killing our mothers; either one or both, a collective murder, so to speak. Instead, we opted to move back in with them. A cooperative apartment here, roughly equivalent to a condominium in the West, costs too much, 5,000 rubles at least."

"You can always try to go abroad," Marina Nikolaevna told Oleg.

"I am surprised you are discussing all this in my presence, after all I'm a foreigner," I said.

"Why? What do we have to lose?" Oleg said. "The paranoia in this country about foreigners is sheer madness." He added, "Besides, Jessica told me that you are a librarian. You might be able to help me with my research project, this is why I told Jessica to invite you."

"What's your research about?" I asked Oleg.

"Let's eat first and I'll tell you later," Oleg replied. I glanced at Marina Nikolaevna eating her chicken. She tore her last piece with her hands and after eating the final tiny bit, she licked her fingers trying to catch all the sauce. She helped herself to some bread, dipping it in the remaining sauce. Then she wiped her mouth clean with a napkin.

Satisfied, Marina Nikolaevna turned her face to the

sun and stretched out her fingers to catch the rays coming through the window. At the same time, she glanced leisurely over the adjacent rooftops. Oleg literally ran to the kitchen again and returned carrying strong tea and biscuits. He was pale now, as if from too much work.

Oleg did not rest when we finished eating. He rose once more, this time to take away the empty plates back to the kitchen. Jessica and I tried to help, but Marina Nikolaevna turned to Jessica and stopped her, exclaiming, "What a lovely sweater! Did you knit it yourself?"

Jessica laughed. "Even if I wanted to, I wouldn't have had the time. I'm a student, you know, I'm very busy with my work."

"And your boots, where did you buy them?"

As the two women talked, I followed Oleg, carrying several plates in my hands. Again we passed the curtain, the stuffy room, the gloomy corridor. A waiting line had formed by one of the doors, which remained closed. It was the toilet. Soon we arrived at the apartment's communal kitchen.

Seven rectangular tables stood wedged against the walls with four ovens in between; no cupboards. The floor was covered in light gray linoleum. The high walls were equally gray. Each table had an iron hook on its side holding a few towels. There was one sink with two taps. Seven enormous dented metal basins used for bathing hung along the walls. The smell was suffocating.

Six of the tables were immaculate. The seventh, Oleg's, was covered with pots, pans and cutlery. I went to the nearby table to lay down the plates without thinking. Oleg said, annoyed, "Laura, pile the dishes on my table. Find a spot there. I'm not allowed to use the other tables."

An older man came in as I rearranged things on the cluttered surface. Oleg addressed him politely, almost deferentially, "I'll be doing the dishes soon, don't worry." The man nodded, looked around while pacing up and down and then decided to leave.

"Who's that?" I asked.

"The head of our collective, a party representative. He supervises the common areas: the kitchen, the corridor, the bathroom, the separate toilet. He doesn't like dishes lying around; he wants them done as soon as possible. We have to be careful to avoid fights here."

Oleg washed the dishes. "I want your opinion about our research project; I'm studying the sociology of sports at the moment," he said. "In our country we have major Olympic athletes, children who begin training early because the parents have party credentials. But the vast majority of our adolescents don't practice any sport, they're uninterested. My research team is working on a questionnaire to figure out ways to increase high school students' motivation. We know the relationship between physical activity and mental health. But we don't really know if it affects boys and girls differently."

"This is a fairly easy problem to deal with," I replied. "Have you gone to your library to research information on authors from other countries who have written on this subject?"

"I can only look up the information from Eastern European countries. The other stacks are closed to me."

"That's unbelievable!"

"But it's still true. With my low rank at the institute, I've limited access to data. It's very frustrating. This is why I need to talk to foreigners, to know what's going on."

"I was never interested in either sports or health; I don't know a lot about those subjects." As I finished the phrase, I feared I had frustrated Oleg further.

After piling the leftovers on one plate, I washed my hands at the second tap in the sink, then I grabbed a nearby towel. Oleg stopped me again, but this time he was rather upset. Maybe I had, indeed, disappointed him with my answer. "Listen, I already told you that you can use only my things. Get that towel over there," he said, pointing with soapy fingers.

"How thoughtless of me! I forgot," I answered, starting to dry the dishes. "Your attitude towards foreigners is different from that of all the others I've met here. Tell me something. Why all the big secrecy about meeting foreigners?"

"People at the top, the party, fear the influence from abroad. I've already been visited by the KGB several times. I'm being watched, but I couldn't care less. It might seem suicidal, but I don't give a damn. My life is not that good, anyway. What can I lose? My share of this apartment? My stupid job?"

Almost instinctively, Oleg approached a small window near the sink. Hiding himself near the wall, he leaned forward and stared at the street below. I assumed that he was searching for a KGB agent standing opposite the building's main entrance; someone might have followed Jessica and me into the apartment.

"Even if you don't care, aren't you afraid of these people?" I asked.

"I run a constant risk, but I try to cover myself. I told my boss that I was meeting you, that I wanted to discuss our project."

"I'm terribly sorry that, as a librarian, I know mostly how to search sources. That's what my work at the Georgetown Public Library in Washington entailed." I wished Oleg were researching, for instance, socio-cultural differences between developed and underdeveloped countries, I had some UNESCO books on that topic at home.

I paused and then asked out of curiosity, "What did your boss say about our meeting?"

"He told me to make a note in our daily register that I was going out to cover a story for our newspaper. Now, with Andropov in power, we record our entering and exit hours at all times. We post new information on our walls regularly and need to leave the institute to run errands once in a while."

"I see."

"My boss is a good fellow; he tries to help me. He sees how depressed I am these days."

Oleg looked at the dish he was washing and paused, "But he's a member of the old school. His work is old-fashioned, ineffective, useless. He doesn't keep up with what's going on outside the country."

"It must be stifling."

"It's killing me. I can't think independently. I was different before; now I feel amorphous, aimless. Above all, I need to please my boss. To survive at the institute I need to agree constantly, to become invisible, to fly low, very low."

Jessica came in. She looked at Oleg. "Sorry for leaving you alone. First, I had to answer all your mother's questions about my clothes. Then, she inquired about the U.S., my family, my parents' house. She is such a curious lady. Then, she had a plan. You divorce Yelena, marry me, and we settle in the U.S. What an imagination she has! After that, I stood in line to use the toilet for over seven minutes."

As she talked, Jessica took a towel from the hook near Oleg's table to help with the dishes.

"Did my mother really say that?" Oleg asked in disbelief. "Did she say that she wanted me to divorce Yelena? Are you sure?"

"Yes. But, maybe, she was kidding, I don't know."

Oleg's eyes reddened, his face flushed. He continued with the dishes, but his anxiety returned. Suddenly he broke a glass in the sink, maybe on purpose. We helped him clean up the mess. When we finished, we realized Oleg had cut his right thumb. "I must hurry up now," he muttered. "With cooking, I've already been out for more than two hours."

We finished up the dishes without speaking any more.

Jessica made two piles of plates and placed the pots, glasses, and cutlery on a tray. The three of us carried everything back to Oleg's rooms.

As we came in, Oleg placed his pile on the table and went straight to his mother. She was doing her nails while sitting in the chair by the bay window, the sunshine still pouring over her. From behind, he clamped his hands around her wrinkled neck. "You know, instead of killing myself, or letting *them* get me, I might kill you," he said. "I might even throw you out of your bay window. What I can't figure out is why you provoke me to deal with you sooner rather than later."

The old lady did not utter a sound. With bulging eyes, she looked imploringly at Jessica while struggling to remove Oleg's hands. But Oleg would not let go. The muscles of his hands were shaking, his teeth clenched. I could see red marks growing round Marina Nikolaevna's neck, close to her son's hands. Blood from his thumb spurted over the collar of her dress. I wished again I could have helped Oleg with his research project. He was delirious with rage, and maybe he felt that he had cooked all that food for nothing. And his mother had eaten most of it.

At that moment Jessica screamed, incredulous to be a witness in such a scene. She rushed to Oleg and beat him boldly on the back. Surprised by her strength, Oleg bent forward and let go of his mother. Straightening himself, he then addressed Jessica and me, shouting in a wild, hollow-sounding voice, "Come on, let's go. I'm already late."

We sped down the stairs, and Oleg disappeared quickly into the street. As we approached Prospket Marx Metro Station and I looked at the red communist banner again, the one about Moscow becoming the ideal city, I said to Jessica, "I'm afraid it's going to take time, in fact, quite some time, before Moscow becomes a 'model city' worth remembering."

Jessica heard me, but she remained silent, still too stunned to speak.

Flames for a Revolution

The day before November 7, Keith and I drove from Helsin-ki through Novgorod on our way to Moscow. As a diplomat with the American Embassy, Keith was allowed to bring a new foreign car into the Soviet Union. For us, it was a splen-did opportunity to see the arrangements for the upcoming celebrations of the October Revolution in that part of the country. According to the day observed by the Gregorian calendar, the festivities always fell on November 7.

En route back to Moscow, we saw quite unexpected expressions of communist fervor. Along the roads hung red flags, red posters, and red banners. On one side of the main square in Novgorod stood a huge placard with pic-tures of various members of the city's central committee. On the other side, equally large, stood an enormous picture of communism's three most celebrated heroes: Marx, Engels, and Lenin.

By the time we reached Moscow the commemorations had already started in the city. As we passed Gorky Street a gigantic picture of Lenin appeared on a building, encircled by flashing red lights. All the surrounding streets had been embellished with red flags placed in metal hooks sticking out of most building facades. The flags flapped in the wind, sounding like an orchestra that followed us all the way home in our new car. The Soviets must have rushed because we had not seen any flags when we left. The job seemed almost routine, like a practice performed year after year, since the days of the Revolution.

Bolshaya Ordynka, where we lived, led into the embankment near Red Square, the country's major celebration site. The activity around our apartment started in the early hours of November 7. People with cheerful faces stepped out of endless buses parked in the vicinity and made their way towards the square. Most carried small red flags, just red, nothing else. It seemed there was no need to embroider the golden hammer and sickle on the upper left corner, as it was in the full-size flag.

As I looked out our apartment window I said to Keith, "It's amazing how happy the Soviets look today."

"This is the main Soviet holiday, Laura. People don't have to go to work; they even get free rides to Red Square."

The average Soviet expected, rightfully, a few exceptional happenings on this special day: the celebration of the victory of communism, the tribute to Lenin's memory, the military parade and, finally, the view of all the Politburo members lined up by the specially erected wooden tribune on top of Lenin's mausoleum.

This happened but once a year.

As Keith and I did not feel like elbowing our way through the crowds in Red Square, we sat on the sofa and watched the celebrations on television. It would be easier to take a stroll after the ceremonies were over.

Television was a superb medium to help intensify people's patriotism. It kept viewers in a state of alert, as if their country was at risk of imminent foreign invasion. Announcers constantly referred to their *rodina*, the motherland, a feminine word in Russian, as a land different from other nations. They told Soviet citizens that they stood apart—after all, they had produced not only a unique revolution but had also played a major role in helping the European powers defy the Nazis in the Second World War.

It was easy to imagine that the Bolshevik Revolution had happened only the week before.

Keith and I decided to go out when the ceremonies ended on television. The November day was almost warm for Moscow, the sky even showing patches of blue amidst enormous white clouds. Hordes of orderly citizens were already returning from Red Square. As we walked briskly along, I pointed at a few cheerful groups.

"Look at those people over there, Keith." I indicated a group carrying a huge red banner. "Listen to how loudly they're singing."

"See how every man has a *znachok*," he answered pointing to one of the characteristic communist lapel badges.

Children ran helter-skelter ahead and behind the groups, excited by the atmosphere. The joyful feeling of a party, not yet over, was still in the air. Keith and I felt drawn into this lively atmosphere.

Again, I turned to Keith, "I feel almost happy today."

"Good, Laura, enjoy it. You don't seem to feel that way very often here."

"People seem so light-hearted. It's contagious."

"I know." Keith put his arm around my shoulders.

"Somehow life seems manageable today."

"I'm glad you can enjoy this country if only for a few hours," he said, clearly relieved by my good mood.

In ten minutes we were in Red Square.

The square was surrounded by portable metal fences brought in for the occasion. Placed at regular intervals, they provided the strategic entrance points into the large open space. After showing our diplomatic cards to the *militsioner* closest to the Moscow River Bridge, we got in quickly. Pushing against the crowds still coming out, we headed in the direction of Lenin's tomb. We wanted to be near the country's central Soviet symbol.

The large crowd had dwindled but there were still

groups of people strolling and talking, showing children the honor guard marching stiffly back and forth, enjoying the sense of space. A feeling of relaxation prevailed.

We saw a few friends from the diplomatic community and started to chat. My friend Ellen, married to Peter Thompson, came to greet us. "How was your trip?" she asked.

"Great, we finally have a car. We had a wonderful lunch in Novgorod yesterday!"

"What was so wonderful about it?"

"Oh, we found a restaurant near the monument dedicated to one thousand years of Russian history and shared a table with two Soviet college students. We discussed literature, Gogol, and Russian absurdities."

"Changing subjects: did you hear that the General Secretary didn't attend the celebrations? Ellen asked, and then continued, "No Soviet broadcast mentioned it."

"That figures," I answered. "What did you expect? That the Soviets disclose Andropov is at death's door?"

"It's only the second or third time since the Revolution that a General Secretary hasn't attended the October celebrations. It's definitely unusual."

We continued chatting casually, until Keith, who had been talking to Peter, suggested that we return home. We said good-bye to our friends and turned our backs to the mausoleum. But, at that precise moment, a rush of people pressed toward the monument, and we heard loud screams. We looked on in awe.

Close by, just a few steps to the right of the mausoleum, we saw—horror of horrors—a man on fire. There, before our very eyes! He was small and frail and half naked. And he was on fire.

It was staggering to see a living torch in front of us.

His body was entirely covered, including his face, in a dark-brown substance, no doubt flammable. The dark and loose-fitting rags that covered his pelvis and legs were quickly consumed. The flames traveled at high speed eating material, skin, and bone. After a few minutes, both arms and shoulders, then the torso and head, all leaned forward, as if unable to remain upright. It was noticeable how his right arm and shoulder tilted lower than the left.

Surprisingly, the human torch made no sound—there was no shouting, no crying, nothing. The screams we heard came from the people around us.

I could smell the scorched flesh, something I had never experienced before. Distracted by the odor, I was not sure how much time had elapsed. Foreigners and Soviets alike stood still, as if glued to the ground; everyone was so shocked that we all seemed paralyzed.

Suddently, a black Volga darted from the side of the square where the GUM department store was located. Mere steps from us, the burning body crumpled to the ground, arms and legs folded in a small circle. Five men dressed in civilian clothes spun out of the car and rushed towards the circular pile, still a human body. With a fire extinguisher and a few light gray blankets they put the flames out.

Their gestures were efficient, resolute, brutal.

And still no sound, no sound whatsoever, came from that body—no shouting, no crying, nothing.

Was the man still alive?

The body was swiftly carried to the car and thrown onto the floor in the back. The men, no doubt policemen in disguise, kicked it repeatedly to adjust it in place. Afterwards, two of them sat in the front, and three were in the back with their feet on top of the body. As the Volga sped across Red Square, those who had not witnessed the scene could not have noticed anything peculiar about the car. The policemen had not placed the body in the trunk, I suspected, to make sure that, if still alive, it could not escape.

Keith and I returned to our group of friends; they talked nervously, unable to leave, pretending that the unsolicited vision, which no one wanted to acknowledge or confront, had not occurred. Maybe we all had had a bad dream, totally outside our realm of former experiences, collective nevertheless, as the Soviets so much enjoyed.

At once, all of us, Soviets and foreigners alike, were surrounded by KGB agents in civilian clothes. We were unable to figure out how they had arrived so quickly.

The KGB bureaucrats were distinct—and dressed differently from regular Soviets. The shoes, the stylish clothing, the warm, comfortable overcoats, were all exclusive marks of their elite status. Also giving them away were the well-washed faces, the trimmed beards, the good haircuts. And they were all fat, as someone accurately observed, even beefy.

They had thin wires running along their broad chests inside their overcoats, and reaching the woolen scarves around their necks. What ordinary Soviet would be carrying that kind of portable radio?

My throat dry with tension, I examined their air of authority, stern expressions, and steady eyes. One Soviet standing not far from me talked excitedly to a group of people eager to hear what had happened. He was quickly taken away with a KGB officer on each side.

Ellen's husband, Peter, had had a chance to take a picture of the small figure in flames. I had seen him positioning himself for the shot. The human torch was in the center. In the background, by the Kremlin wall, hung a poster showing a group of smiling Soviet workers talking to peasant girls.

"Give me your film," said one beefy KGB agent approaching Peter.

"This is my camera," Peter replied.

The man did not lose a beat but looked Peter in the eye and said, "Give me your film, or I will take your camera."

"Why?"

"These are my orders," was the agent's reply.

Peter exposed the film himself instead of fighting or giving his own camera to the man.

Other agents came closer trying to hear what our group was saying. A well-built man and a woman stood near us pretending to talk to each other. I noticed the good clothing, the polished shoes, the clean features. Seconds later the man came toward our group while his friend took a picture of us.

Irked, Peter addressed the man, "Come closer. Why don't you stand in the middle? This picture with all of us might earn you the Order of Lenin. What a great honor!"

The fellow smiled stupidly.

The glances between our group and the agents detailed the hostility of the Cold War itself. Who would vacillate first? Who could stand the pressure longer? Who might strike the next blow? It seemed to go on forever. The KGB agents gazed blankly at us, but remained, indisputably, in charge. We were astonished. A Soviet woman not far from me, disturbed by what she had seen, talked loudly to the people around her. An agent approached and stood by her side. I faced him deliberately. She asked him for an explanation of what had happened—once, twice—but got no answer. After a while, scared by his impassive expression, she became quiet.

Another Soviet man stood near us and talked loudly to himself, "This person had no sense, he could have set the mausoleum on fire. It might have been dangerous for Lenin's body. Who was that man? No Soviet, not one of us, would have done something like that."

The KGB representative left this Soviet to his own monologue.

Our group continued to stand around for a while, talking. Minutes later, Keith and I decided to leave, there was nothing left to do. Keith was a young, low-ranking diplomat, no one bothered to follow us. We walked silently for a while. Carefree people were still all over the place. A couple threw red carnations at each other. Closer to home I asked Keith, "Do you think the human torch didn't want to shout? Or he couldn't?"

"I think he chose not to. He must have planned this for months, if not years," Keith said.

"What about the rotten smell?"

"Something to remember forever."

I felt like one of the rags that the human torch had been wearing. As we continued to walk I added, "I really detest the secrecy in this country."

At home, we did not do much for the rest of the afternoon. Our building had a common furnace, therefore we could not regulate the temperature in our apartment independently. Since the day was not too cold, it was rather hot inside, even stifling. I changed from street clothes into something lighter in the bedroom. All our apartment's windows had been sealed for the winter with cotton and tape, so I could only open the bedroom *fortochka*, the upper windowpane, so small, so typically Russian.

But it did not help. My skin started to itch, my legs were tingling. It was as if I was burning, too.

Abruptly, I started to scratch myself and scratched for hours. Keith was as shocked as I, and that made him rather sympathetic. He held my hands, trying to calm me down, but to no avail. I seemed unable to relax or even take in the bit of cool air that came in through the *fortochka*.

The next morning my legs were covered in red sores, deep marks from my own fingernails.

"Krasnaya Ploshchad," I told Keith, "I know it means Red Square, Beautiful Square, in old Russian. But this square will never be beautiful in my eyes again. Never. Not even in a million years."

"I understand, we saw something awful," Keith said.

"Do you think there's a yearly immolation in front of Lenin's mausoleum? And do you think that, yearly, it goes unreported?" I persisted.

"We'll never find out," Keith replied, still trying to calm down my hands.

Glass Silhouettes

When Keith and I arrived at the American Embassy in Moscow, the initial briefing in the soundproof room was pretty clear. The officer told us that we had to assume that our apartments were bugged. He advised us to keep our troubles to ourselves, that anything told to a Soviet could be used for blackmail. Also, he cautioned us to pay attention to what the Soviets disclosed, it could be of interest to the embassy. Since the Soviets were supposed to report on us to their government, we should not be ashamed.

As Americans and Soviets worked together at the embassy, and as nonworking spouses, like me, spent a lot of time there, the atmosphere easily bred suspicion and anxiety. The situation was worsened by the fact that the embassy had, at the time, over one hundred Soviet employees on whose work the Americans depended. The administrative personnel, repairmen, maids, and chauffeurs were all Soviets.

Like everybody else in the embassy community, I sought a friendly coexistence with the Soviets. But day after day I guarded myself carefully. Pretending to be more adjusted than I really felt, I tried to disguise the difficulties of my new role as a diplomat's wife in a hostile country. I did not plan to disclose anything personal, anything that might be used later against Keith or myself. I was determined, at the same time, to avoid feeling vulnerable.

One day during the initial settling-in period, I planned lunch at the embassy's snack bar with my new French friend, Denise. She was young, green-eyed, beautiful and, like me, recently married to an American. As I had been born in Portugal and both of us had plunged into two foreign cultures at once—Russian and American—we found it easy to relate to each other.

As we walked towards the snack bar in the embassy's decrepit courtyard, I said, "I need some work done in my apartment. Will you come with me to Lyudmila's office? She's so difficult." The system prohibited staff from hiring their own workmen, so Lyudmila held a crucial job controlling the requests for household repairs.

"Is she ever difficult!" Denise burst out. "I need to talk to her, too, the tap in my kitchen sink is leaking. Did you hear about her while you were in Washington?"

"No. What did people say?"

"That it's better to be on her good side. A fight with Lyudmila means trouble, a lot of trouble."

"What do you mean?"

"You don't want the meat in your freezer to spoil or your stove broken for a week, do you?"

"Of course not."

"So be nice to her. Let's go and talk to her now."

We went into Lyudmila's cubicle, a low, prefabricated hut located at the right side of the courtyard. She was standing at the counter by the entrance door as usual. Lyudmila was a petite woman in her early forties, delicately built, thin-faced. She scrutinized us as we entered.

"Hi, Lyudmila, how are you?" Denise greeted her with a broad smile. "Listen, I need a plumber to come to my apartment today. I had to wash the dishes in the bathroom sink last night. If the water continues to leak from the kitchen tap, it might reach the apartment downstairs."

Business-like Lyudmila answered, "You need to fill out

a work order. I don't know when the next crew will be available."

"This is an emergency; I'm worried about a short-circuit, even a flood. Where are the work orders?" Denise asked, reaching for the pile of paper. "You remember me, don't you? I'm a friend of Nora and Thomas Clark. They're in Germany now, and send their greetings to you."

Lyudmila replied sharply, "You already told me that several times. Give me the work order when you finish. And don't forget to sign it."

Denise scribbled her request, her smile gone now. As she handed it to Lyudmila, she added, subdued, "By the way, this is my friend Laura. She needs to fill out a work order too."

Lyudmila turned to me saying, "I remember seeing you here before. Don't tell me what you need; write it down."

This scene was the first of many to follow. The system did not work well, and the repairmen were inefficient. A crew of three men would come to an apartment to fix a tap. One worked, another passed tools, and the third stared at the wall. A couple of days later—poor materials, faulty workmanship, no one could tell—the tap would break again. It was necessary to return to Lyudmila and fill out another work order; later, another crew, that did not know what the previous one had done, was dispatched. It never ended.

Mired in a sea of requests, Lyudmila's gloom intimidated all, particularly the embassy wives. I was no exception. Once in a while I tried to crack a joke or comment on the weather. But nothing worked. It was a lucky day when Nina, her assistant, filled in for her. Nina had bangs, always a smile on her lips and wore tight jeans. We all knew she loved to watch Westerns.

A few weeks later, Lyudmila passed me in the courtyard with a bunch of papers in her hand. I tried praising the system, "Hi, Lyudmila, I've just come from home. The four workmen in my apartment are doing a great job. They might finish installing the carpet in the next half hour."

"Did you say four people are there? I only sent three."

"You did? Who is the fourth one, then?"

"I don't know."

"How come? You gave the workmen the extra set of keys so they could come in if I was out. I thought the fourth man was the supervisor and that's why they were working so quickly."

Lyudmila remained silent. I stared at her, "Will you find out what that fourth man is doing in the apartment?"

"If I remember. If I have the time. I need to go now. Good-bye."

I told myself there was nothing to worry about. There were no secrets lying around, anyway. Stealing, I had heard, got repairmen into big trouble. At the embassy, Keith worked on one of the upper floors; to go and talk to him meant passing the security check. He usually did not like my interruptions. So, for the moment, I made an effort to put the issue out of my mind.

As I was returning to the embassy building, Nina came out of the office, smoking. She loved foreign cigarettes and never missed an opportunity to put one in her mouth. Keith and I had hardly talked the previous evening, his mood had been taciturn, so I approached Nina for a bit of distraction.

"Hi, Nina, how's it going?"

"So, so. Lyudmila's in a bad mood today. I don't want her to see me talking to you."

"Why?"

"I just don't, that's all," she puffed the smoke into my face.

"Too bad, I wanted to tell you about a movie I saw recently. It's about...," but before I had a chance to continue, Nina was gone. I turned in the direction of the main building and realized that Lyudmila was watching us through the glass doors. She had her glasses on and her piercing eyes studied us attentively.

Weeks later, in the middle of January, I went to Lyudmila's cubicle again, ready to fill in yet another damn work order. The entrance door could not be properly shut, and inside was as cold as the North Pole. Lyudmila was at the helm, standing by the counter; her face looked like a piece of ice. Her hair was shorter than usual, her ears red with the freezing temperature. To keep her nose dry she held an off-white handkerchief crumpled in her hand. She wore a shabby pale yellow sweater and looked weary; as usual, she wore no make-up.

I tried to be friendly. "Lyudmila, how are you? I hear Nina is having a baby. She surely disguised her pregnancy well."

"Yes, that's right."

"I didn't even know she was married."

"She isn't."

"I didn't know that either. You don't seem happy for her—am I right?" I tried to figure Lyudmila out.

"She's out of her mind, bringing another child into this world with no husband."

"She's a grown woman; she knows what she's doing."

"No, she doesn't. I told her about my case. My parents divorced when I was six months old. Since primary school I've known what it's like to come home to an empty place."

"I'm sorry to hear that. Look, Nina has been rather helpful. I bought a romper for her baby. Will you pass it on to her?"

"I might not see her."

"But if you do, will you give it to her?"

"All right, but don't count on it," she took the gift from my hands.

I left disturbed. Something about Lyudmila bothered me. Trying to win her over was no use, I knew that already.

But I sensed a feeling of deep deprivation, as if Lyudmila lacked something fundamental, something at her very core. Life working for an enemy embassy, although a prestigious job, had not given her the least bit of happiness.

Nina's small present was a strategy to ease embassy tension. Gifts like the romper were modest but required preparation. When abroad on vacation, I stocked up for the next holidays—women's stockings, always large sizes, shampoos, make-up. These items brought a lot of good will among the Soviet staff since the country was permanently undersupplied.

One day, while wrapping a few presents for International Women's Day, a big Soviet holiday, I realized to my dismay that I had forgotten Lyudmila in my list. She was too thin for the stockings and too serious for the make-up or the shampoo. Moreover, I wanted to give her something personal, something special that might touch her on a deeper level but without my appearing frivolous in her eyes.

Looking around the apartment, my eyes paused on the miniature crystal animals displayed in the china cabinet. I had almost a complete zoo: a rabbit, a cat, a dog, a rhinoceros, an elephant, even a giraffe. The pieces were attractive with black eyes and bent tails blown in well-cut, refined glass. I had found a present for Lyudmila. I would give her the rabbit, as it was the cuddliest of all the animals. I wrapped it in colorful paper. The following day I offered it to her, with my good wishes for the success of women in her country.

In the Soviet manner, Lyudmila thanked me but did not open the gift in my presence. To my delight, however, I realized a few weeks later that she was pleased. For once, she smiled when I addressed her with a new work order.

From that time on, it was my pleasure to give her yet another glass animal when a holiday came. As the months followed, Lyudmila was becoming more cordial. When I entered her office one day, fresh from a week abroad, she said, "I heard you and your husband were on vacation. Did you have a good time?"

"We had a great time," I lied to Lyudmila. "And I loved Italy—the food, the monuments, the colorful streets. Who told you we were away?"'

"Christina Miller, the lady who arrived last month, you seem good friends with her. I sent the crew to your apartment to fix the dryer. Have you tried it yet?"

"No, we returned last night."

"How do you plan to use your time now that you're back?" Lyudmila took off her glasses and cleaned them; I took her gesture as a device to probe at me.

"I still haven't figured that out. The kinds of embassy jobs offered to spouses don't appeal to me. And, there isn't a single library in Moscow that will hire me. Not even as a volunteer."

"That's true, we give our jobs to our own people." Lyudmila said as she put her glasses back on. She proceeded: "We all see your husband working after hours all the time, he strikes us as an ambitious fellow."

I sighed unexpectedly as I said, "I know," but Lyudmila's expression remained composed. I continued, "I came by because one of the bathroom taps is leaking. I need to fill out a work order."

"Here," Lyudmila gave me the form.

"Thanks a lot." I filled in the request.

Our vacation had provided the Soviets with the perfect opportunity to inspect everything in our home, such as checking whether the bugs were working properly. But at least Lyudmila was approachable now, sometimes even affable. I wondered whether the crew reported its findings to her. If so, what did she do with the information? I had never found out who the fourth man in the apartment had been that day of the carpet installation.

The collection I was gradually giving her had been a wedding present from a relative who knew I loved animals. As time went on, I watched Keith when he passed the china cabinet to see if he noticed the missing animals. Sure enough one evening he asked, "Do you think the maid is stealing our glass menagerie?"

"Oh no, not at all. I've been giving the miniatures to Lyudmila, and she's much nicer these days."

"Why are you giving her these presents?"

"I discovered that she likes animals."

"Why didn't you ask if I minded?"

"You're always so busy that we hardly talk. And you aren't as fond of animals."

"Didn't you think they might have sentimental value to me?"

"We can easily replace them when we return to the U.S. Besides, since I'm the one who deals with Lyudmila, I needed a way to her heart."

"We've just been on vacation, you could have told me."

"We spent so much time arguing that I forgot!"

Keith dropped the issue.

One day we got an invitation to a dinner party from Richard Myers, one of Keith's colleagues. Keith drove to the party silently; after a full day's work these dinners were an extension of his job. I imagined Keith was reviewing the guest list in his mind; he always studied it beforehand. The party promised to be exciting since several actors from the Taganka Theater, the most daring group in Moscow, had been invited. I was sorry that my friend Christina was not attending the party. She had left Moscow within twenty-four hours the previous week, for her husband had been declared persona non grata by the Soviet government.

At Richard's apartment a large group of Americans and Soviets were talking in the living area. Someone played Scott Joplin on the piano. Many American Embassy Soviet employees were also there; they loved to be invited by the American diplomats, it proved that they were liked, respected. The atmosphere was easy-going with a lot of food laid out on the dining-room table. Keith introduced himself to one of the artists, a man stunningly dressed in a dark green velvet outfit. They started to talk. Finding myself alone, I joined Denise—she had also been invited—and a group of Soviets in the living room.

Later on, I followed my group into the dining room, where I saw Lyudmila. She looked great that evening in a patterned skirt, a cotton yellow shirt, and a navy blazer, her eye make-up visible through her thick glasses. With Christina in mind and not wanting to put on a facade that day, I turned away from Lyudmila deliberately.

While I was having dessert, Lyudmila came over. Somehow, I felt threatened and scanned the room for Keith. He was talking to a group in the living room, one of the men had a funny expression, and I imagined him to be mimicking a public figure.

"Laura, it's good to see you," Lyudmila exclaimed pleasantly, a glass of wine in her hand.

"Good seeing you, too, Lyudmila. What's up?"

"I wanted to tell you that Nina had a baby boy, and I've given her the romper."

"I was afraid you might forget."

"I didn't. Sometimes I get bitchy at work, as you know, but I carry such a heavy load." Lyudmila sounded apologetic, I could not believe my ears. I was so surprised that I did not reply.

"The food tonight is delicious, as usual. Did you try the *borshch*, our marvelous beet soup? I love Richard, he always invites me. And you know what, I've been meaning to tell you for a long time," Lyudmila said as she dragged me aside, "I like you very much, too."

"You're full of compliments tonight, aren't you?"

"I'll tell you why I like you," Lyudmila's voice lowered as she said this. She took off her thick glasses and looked closely into my eyes. "You're so different from the other wives I handle. You're a European like us."

"Thank you," I replied, mistrustful of her associating me with the Soviets. Where was Lyudmila heading? Why had she taken off her glasses?

"I also love the animal collection you gave me. Such pretty things," she continued animatedly.

"Stop it, you're embarrassing me," I answered, realizing that Lyudmila meant what she was saying. I was so taken aback that I placed the dessert plate on the table, it seemed too heavy to hold.

"I have a poodle, a present from my former American boss and his wife. I call him Nutka, a combination I made of their two first names put together. I suspect you like animals, too."

"I really do," I replied, trying to keep up my smile.

"I adore my dog, such company, such comfort. Our walks together mean a lot to me. People in the street stop me and ask for an explanation of the animal's unusual name. I love it!" Lyudmila gulped some more wine. She had not put her glasses on yet.

"With your busy schedule how do you manage to walk Nutka?" I asked, amused by the dog's name.

"I make time. I walk him every morning before going to work, and as soon as I return in the evening."

"Even in the deep of winter?"

"Of course. I get up at four-thirty, by five I'm already out. In the evening, I rush home to walk him before I do my shopping."

"Wow!" I saw a nightmare in front of me: Lyudmila making it through the snow, her knees frozen, the dog by the leash.

"I have to do what it takes. Also, Nutka sleeps with me.

It's so cozy."

"How nice." I felt moved by Lyudmila's confession.

"Why don't you get a dog yourself, Laura? You might like it as much as a dear friend. Who knows? You might like it even more than your husband." Lyudmila said this with a short laugh, her voice still low, her eyes still eating me up. "It isn't good to feel lonely."

"How do you know I feel lonely?" I felt like a glass silhouette myself. Was Lyudmila forcing a personal admission? Or did she want my view on Christina's abrupt departure, since I was sure she knew about it? Was I not even allowed the solace of my private misery? Gathering energy, I heard myself asking, "Why do you think a dog would be good for me?"

She answered my second question. "Because a dog is great company. Much friendlier, much warmer than most human beings. Don't you agree?"

"I'll think about it." I tried to sound light. Feeling exposed, I looked for Keith again, but he was still busy with his group.

"There's something else," Lyudmila added eagerly.

"What?" I quickly asked, afraid now. Here was Lyudmila, the embassy terror, exchanging secrets with me.

"Take the animals you gave me, they're the best of friends. They don't even require any work." After she said this, Lyudmila put her glasses back on, maybe she felt she did not need to inspect me any longer.

But I felt my throat all clogged up as I sensed Lyudmila's sincerity. Animals, instead of human beings, had, indeed, been the key to her heart. I replied only, "You're right, you're absolutely right." Lyudmila was so absorbed by her confessions that she did not seem to notice my disquiet. She had finished her glass of wine.

"Sometimes in the evening, with Nutka in my lap, I sit down in my room and admire my zoo. Such fine company."

Her voice was not only low now, it had depth too.

As Lyudmila kept on talking, I could not stand it any longer. After a long journey, I had found a way to comfort her; it was unbearably risky, however, to let Lyudmila comfort me. Saying clumsily "Lyudmila, excuse me, I need to go now," I left Lyudmila alone.

Border Crossing

Twice a year Keith and I took the diplomatic mail pouch from the American Embassy in Moscow to Helsinki, Finland. These trips were fun, and free—with the possibility of staying abroad for a couple of days. Months ahead of time we listed our availability on the embassy's roster. Trips during the winter months, offering an escape from Moscow's cold drudgery, were particularly desirable. In order to cross Soviet territory, we had to fill out various forms for the Ministry of Foreign Affairs, stating our itinerary, date of departure and date of arrival. Helsinki was as cold as Moscow, but a blessing of sorts. At night, the colors of neon signs were everywhere; the restaurants offered fresh vegetables and smiling clerks; and the city had brand name shops like Marimekko, whose bright fabrics made the snow-covered ground glitter.

On one occasion there was a train strike while we were still in Helsinki. Instead of traveling back to Moscow by train, as usual, we took a bus. It was late April but it was still wet with bits of snow swirling everywhere.

As the bus moved eastward on the modern Finnish highway, I looked out the window at the surrounding marshes. Although I was enjoying the landscape, and carried a diplomatic passport, I still felt uneasy about crossing the border near Vyborg, in the Soviet Union.

The bus was filled with both Soviets and foreigners. As

we approached the border, I noticed that everyone looked tense. The passengers had stopped talking and now whispered to each other instead. I wondered if they felt as apprehensive as I did; and whether entering Soviet territory would be as troublesome as it usually was by train or by plane.

I dreaded the Soviet border guards—every single one of them. Unlike Keith, diplomatic by nature and conviction, I did not take their conduct in stride. Their eagerness and over-zealous devotion to their job appalled me. I recollected how, one day, I had a two-inch plastic flowerpot on the train windowsill and a guard told me I could not bring foreign soil into Russia. My protests at their inspections were usually met with a disapproving sneer. When I spoke out Keith remained neutral, uninvolved, and that made me angrier.

With plenty of time on my hands, I found myself rather surprised at my thoughts. In Helsinki, I unexpectedly missed the constant references to Lenin made by the Soviets. In Moscow, Lenin was everywhere: in squares and shops, in people's speech, and on television. In Helsinki it was different. Squares had other monuments, shops had other busts, and everybody appeared cheerful.

I interrupted Keith, who was reading Richard Pipes' *Russia Under the Old Regime* and tried to find some comfort, "Keith, listen, this is amazing. I felt conditioned to expect a statue of Lenin in every square I crossed in Helsinki. I was almost disappointed when I didn't find them. Did the same thing happen to you?"

"Well, yes, in a way," Keith put the book aside for a moment. "I didn't forget the Soviet system in two days. Helsinki is totally different, but I knew I was going back to Moscow."

"I walked in the square near the harbor and was surprised to see only boats."

"I can see that."

"It's scary. If I leave Moscow for two days, and I'm already missing Lenin, this means that I can get used to anything—almost anything."

"After Moscow, you need to spend a lot of time abroad to forget the system."

With these words Keith finished the conversation and returned to his book. Unable to chat more as I had wanted, I decided to read, too. I had with me a book about Lenin and his love for children that was part of an illustrated Soviet series entitled *My First Books*. But still absorbed in my thoughts, I held the book in my lap, unopened.

A middle-aged Soviet couple sat in the seats in front of us; they were unusually well dressed, well-mannered people. The woman now got up to stretch her legs and, as if by accident, bent over to see what I was reading. When I looked at her, she immediately turned away.

The reading was enjoyable. One of the stories described how Lenin went to lunch at a friend's house. When the children did not eat everything their mother placed on their plates, Lenin would not admit them into the "Collective of the Clean Plates." It was only after they promised to conform—amidst great smiles—that he granted them entrance. The children wrote a declaration, and Lenin distributed *znachki*, characteristic lapel buttons in the country.

The merits of collectivism did not last long with me. The bus was slowing down, a sign that we were approaching the border. I joined the other passengers looking out of windows. The marshes had given way to a dense forest filled with gigantic pine and birch trees. A small house appeared, and a man outside it waved. He was a Finnish customs officer, not even wearing a uniform. He smiled at the bus driver and, somehow, his calm greeting warmed my heart.

Keith was still reading his book, but I ventured, "We're getting to the border, don't you want to stop reading and look out?"

"You're interrupting me," he said, impatiently.

"Yes, I am, I thought you might want to look out."

"What is there to see?"

"Soon we'll be at the border, it'll be interesting."

"Let me finish this page. And don't interrupt me again."

"You and your books, it's always the same, we can never talk."

"You're getting angry, aren't you?"

"Yes, I am. It's amazing how history is a substitute for day-to-day reality for you. It helps to cover up your feelings."

As I said this, I opened our picnic dinner and started to eat. I needed the nourishment, as much for physical as emotional reasons. When Keith finished his page, I offered him a sandwich. As usual, he ate slowly, swallowing carefully. When he finished, I asked, "Do you want another one? Customs might be a drag, we might be held up for quite a while."

"No need to make too much of it. One is plenty for now."

"What about a piece of fruit?"

"I can wait."

I continued looking out the window as we passed two checkpoints. A worn-out metal plaque with the inscription CCCP, the equivalent in the Cyrillic alphabet of USSR, announced that we were entering the Soviet Union. The scene at the first guardhouse we passed repeated itself as if rehearsed a thousand times. Two uniformed guards stood by their small, yellow guardhouse, obstructing the road with their bodies. Behind them a primitive iron gate further blocked our passage. The gates seemed so fragile that a child could knock them down. After waiting a few minutes, an old-fashioned traffic light turned from red to green, and one of the guards opened the gate for the bus to pass.

The landscape appeared desolate now. All the traffic—cars, buses, trucks—was heading in one direction, from Finland into the Soviet Union. For me, a huge prison lay ahead. It was already getting late in the afternoon, and the surrounding grayness did not help my state of mind. The road seemed an interminable tunnel into Dostoyevsky's hell.

Soon the bus reached a house with a large sign on top, *Tamozhnya*. We had arrived at the customs house. It was old, faded yellow, and dilapidated. The long, vertical windows were so dirty that it was difficult to see inside. Uniformed guards stood everywhere. One of them directed our bus driver to a stop. Nearby, a trench had been dug—a few feet long and maybe three feet wide—only large enough for a broad-shouldered man to walk through. At night, it would be easy to inadvertently fall into it.

A young, blond guard boarded the bus and, in Russian, asked passengers to bring all their belongings inside. "We have two suitcases to carry, plus our handbags. Let's leave the plastic bag here, it shouldn't make any difference," I said to Keith, referring to a plastic bag containing last minute shopping: Mozart's *Great Mass in C Minor*, a few bars of chocolate, and two or three newspapers.

"That'll be fine," was Keith's only answer.

The customs house was smoggy. It reeked of an unpleasant mixture of unwashed bodies, cigarette butts, and cheap beer. Mildew clung to the walls. Keith and I queued up at one of the control booths, awaiting our turn. When I got closer, I realized that the attendant was barely seventeen years old, he did not even have the first traces of a beard. His resolute eyes, however, contrasted sharply with Lenin's idealistic children.

When my turn came, I slipped my passport through a small glass opening in the booth. The counter was high. I could hardly see the youngster's face beneath his olive green and brown hat, but he could see my movements from head to toe through a thin, horizontal mirror placed on the booth's ceiling. After looking at my passport, he called someone with a question, probably checking my itinerary. While he waited for an answer, he inspected the passport pages. I looked at the line where over twenty people stood waiting. When he hung up the phone, he studied my picture.

"Look at me," he commanded, staring into my eyes.

I did, grimacing.

"What is your name?" he inquired.

"*Molodoy chelovek,*" I said, looking at him as if I were addressing a waiter in a restaurant, "Young man, are you so young that you cannot read my passport?" I was going to take my revenge one way or another.

No answer.

"Is this picture yours?" he asked now, showing me my own picture on the passport.

"What do you think, *molodoy chelovek*?" I replied, a higher tone to the end of my sentence.

Still no answer. He filled in a few forms and told me to move on. It was Keith's turn now. As he approached the booth he warned me, "Laura, please, give us a break. I know this is difficult for you. But soon we'll be out of here. Remember, we're traveling home to Moscow. Please."

"I couldn't resist," I answered with a smirk. "I just wanted to show the guard that not everyone loves him like the Soviet state does. That was all."

Recalling the pride the Soviets took in their border guards, the image of the huge firecrackers in Moscow the previous year—the day designated as the "Celebration of the Border Guards' Work"—weighed on me. To feel better, I took out a piece of chocolate I had placed in my pocket before we left the bus.

After Keith passed the booth, diligently answering the guard's questions, we waited for the other passengers at one side of the room. The guards' inspection of tourists and Soviet citizens alike was painful to watch. Every single suitcase was opened, layer after layer carefully inspected. Handbags were turned upside down—cosmetics, cameras, and books meticulously checked. Some guards took notes as they went along, writing down every possible item.

Uncomfortable, I went outside as I had noticed several guards around our bus. A few people followed, including the well-dressed Russian woman who sat in front of me on the bus. She seemed hurried, walking straight ahead, and her husband followed, as if she were leading a party of two.

A team of guards inside the bus slowly checked the rows of seats, one by one. A different team, using flashlights, examined the bus outside, the motor cubicle, the luggage compartments, and behind the wheels. To my astonishment, two men jumped into the trench and a guard asked the driver to move the bus over it. With the men starting at opposite ends, the flashlights worked the undercarriage like a military operation, one inch at a time.

While watching the inspection, the Russian couple talked to each other in earnest. I noticed that the wife was wearing black, high-heeled shoes. The heels were not only high but quite thick. And although the woman seemed perfectly normal physically, only the front part of her right shoe touched the ground, not her heel. The heel seemed to have a life of its own. It was raised high, as far away from the ground as possible. This odd posture elevated her right knee, leg, upper body, and shoulder.

She seemed totally out of balance. And she spoke nonstop, though quietly, to her husband. He remained composed, only nodding his head in agreement. Her stress was evident in her foot, as if the heel alone dared to show her feelings.

Keith joined me and I said, "Look how disturbed our bus neighbor seems. Look at her right heel, how high it is.

I would give anything to hear what she's muttering to her husband."

"She does seem upset."

"Do you think she's smuggling, that she has something hidden in the heel of her shoe?"

"Laura, what an imagination. I don't think so."

"What is going on, then? If we come closer, they'll stop talking. So I don't think we will ever find out."

"Maybe she has dozens of German marks glued to her sole."

"There you go again."

"Maybe diamonds? Maybe cocaine?"

"Laura, stop. We'll never know. This conversation is useless."

"Oh, God, look, a team of two guards is approaching them. Oh, no!" I shouted.

Two busy-looking men summoned the couple. We could not hear what they were saying, but the woman's heel came down instantly. Seconds later, she and her husband carried their suitcases back inside. The guards followed closely.

"What's going on?" I asked Keith, definitely upset now.

"How would I know, Laura? Be reasonable, alright?"

"Something is going on, something that truly escapes me, and you want me to be reasonable!"

"Yes, that's exactly what I'm saying. Make an effort."

"I can't. I'm going to follow those people inside." I turned around without waiting for Keith's reply.

The couple and the two guards stood by a closed door. The husband's expression was subdued, while the wife showed deep concern. Unobtrusively, I went closer and looked at her heel again—it was still down on the ground. Her tension was gone, she had been caught.

A few minutes later a door opened; it had no sign on top. A tall, fat guard appeared. His light blue eyes were lifeless, his skin rough, full of tiny red marks. He moved around confidently, and I guessed that he was the head of the station. He motioned them to enter a small room.

The couple stayed inside for a long time—twenty minutes, half an hour, maybe—and my eyes did not leave the closed door for a second. I wanted to open the door and grab the woman, take her away from the interrogation. Could her crime be that vile?

Eventually the door opened and the couple came out, followed by the two guards. The woman's face was blanched, the husband's red. They carried their suitcases again and queued outside to get back onto the bus.

I was watching them when I realized that instead of her black, high-heeled shoes the woman was wearing something else. She had on a kind of *tapochki*, special overshoes which were worn in museums to protect the floors throughout the Soviet Union. They were dark gray, tied with black straps. Freed, she looked like a prisoner.

Keith and I joined the queue. As a guard instructed the passengers to place their bags back into the luggage compartments, the driver opened the front door. Another guard ordered us to hurry because the bus was now behind schedule.

The Soviet couple sat in their seats. As I passed them, I looked the lady in the eye, but she ignored me completely, she did not want any contact.

Still standing by my seat, I noticed that our plastic bag was exactly where I had left it. I took my coat off, sat down, and looked inside the bag. All the newspapers were there, as were the chocolate bars. So was the record we had bought. But the thin cellophane wrapper that had enclosed the record, the mark it was unopened, had vanished. There was no trace of the cellophane wrapper whatsoever, not even the smallest piece. Maybe the job had been done with a pocket-knife or a razor blade.

It was as if no one had touched our record.

In disgust I looked at Keith. He realized what had happened when I pulled one of the records from the sleeve. But he shrugged, saying, "The usual harassment, the usual boorishness; nothing new."

I did not feel like answering. For me it was more than that. I uttered only, "You know, after all, I guess I can't get used to certain things. That's not who I am."

With these words, I tried to get comfortable in my seat and closed my eyes. Unable to fall sleep, I asked Keith after a while, "What do you think happened to the woman's shoes?"

"I have no clue. Perhaps the guards took them away."

"Why?"

"She probably bought them in Helsinki. She was doing something illegal. But they let her go free, so all is well."

"Maybe with you, not with me," I said, as I remembered the endless lines in our neighborhood when shoes appeared for sale in a nearby shop.

As I said this I looked out the window once more. In the distance, several agricultural implements, the mark of an agricultural *kolkhoz*, a collective farm, were visible. As we came closer, the farm's name emerged above the dark iron gate by the road. I read the name in Cyrillic, *Druzhba narodov*, Friendship of Peoples.

After a while I fell asleep, waking up only the following morning with Keith tapping my shoulder. We were already in the bus terminal in Moscow. As we left the bus Keith pointed out, "You seem most distressed, but the truth is that nothing really unusual happened to us."

To which I barely replied, anguished, condescending, "Oh, I know, I know!"

Lost Chance

That Saturday morning I lost the chance to get the only embassy job I had wanted in Moscow. As a diplomat with the American Embassy, Keith often worked late into the evening. I visited sights, studied Russian, and eagerly observed everything around me. Until that fateful morning, applying for a part-time job had always been a possibility. The position I had in mind was as Community Liaison Office Coordinator, a plum. The CLO was a clearing-house of information; besides, it organized activities to help the community maintain morale far from home and assisted newly arrived embassy families to settle in. I was eligible to apply after the mandatory six-month residence. Many overqualified spouses, myself included, were interested in the position. The job was conveniently part-time. Moreover, it gave the coordinator not only the satisfaction of helping others navigate Moscow but also the opportunity to establish, first-hand, new contacts and friendships.

I had befriended—and observed—Bridget, the current CLO coordinator. Her husband was leaving Moscow and the position would soon be open. A reference from her could really help my application.

Bridget was pleasant, and we shared several common interests. She knew the city fairly well, which was a real advantage. Although we were not close friends, we respected each other. Bridget said she liked my openness to new experiences; I admired Bridget demeanor. She was the perfect diplomat's wife, well poised, gracefully spoken.

One day, our mutual friend Rose called, and asked me to join Bridget and her at the Sandunov Baths the following Saturday. These communal baths, the most famous in the city, were a ritual of sorts. For us, to go there was like spending a few hours at a spa. We could choose from a vast array of activities: the swimming pool, the wet and dry parlors, the Turkish bath, and the massage salon. In special rooms, zealous, possibly lecherous women, washed others for an extra fee.

The event was a send-off for Rose, whose life-long dream had come true. She was leaving the next day for Bolivia to bring back a child she and her husband had just adopted.

On Saturday, as the three of us stood in line to enter the baths, we realized that the place was going to be crowded. After buying our tickets, we lined up with all the other women. We were going to the baths for fun, but we knew that for most of the Soviet women it was otherwise; they had come to bathe because the city's communal apartments had too few bathrooms. Chatting away with our toiletry bags in hand, a young Russian ahead of us asked, "You're foreigners, aren't you?"

"Yes, we are," Bridget answered cordially, "We love to come here once in a while."

"All foreigners have bathrooms at home. Why do you come to our public baths?" she persisted, eating her words with envy.

"A good scrub doesn't hurt, does it?" Bridget smiled, oblivious to the woman's tone of voice.

"Foreigners always have the best, while we have to put up with having less," the woman replied.

Bridget looked at her watch, ten to ten, the Sandunov Baths would open soon. We had arrived around nine-thirty. Had we been late, the growing line would have left us not only to the biting cold but, probably, to more bickering.

The line charged in when the doors opened. Women pushed past each other to get to the changing room and their favorite bench as quickly as possible. It was like getting the best table at the neighborhood café in Paris. If you lost it, your only chance was next week. In the rush, armed in their heavy winter coats, the women smashed their bags against each other. At one point, I found myself lifted off my feet. Like a soccer mob, the crowd had no mercy.

The benches in the changing room—where clothing was hung and toiletries laid—were strategic vantage points. The ones far away from the front door were the best because there would not be any drafts while undressing. The ones closer to the old, still elaborate windowpanes provided solace, a return to the past. The clothing hooks on these benches still showed, somehow, their well-polished brass. Other benches were located in such a way as to make access to the inside halls rather easy. This was important because the women using these benches could avoid stepping on carelessly placed sandals, bowls filled with hot water, or pumice stones for rough feet.

Cries of triumph, or dismay, echoed in the room as the women claimed—or lost—their favorite benches. Bridget, Rose, and I managed to settle near the entrance to the inside halls. We needed a bench with three consecutive spaces to be together. After bathing, we would sit down and chat while sipping tea.

A Russian woman came up to me saying, "*Gospozha*, you took our seats." I felt protected, somehow, that she addressed me as "lady," she had not used *tovarishch*, comrade. For sure she knew we were foreigners. "Those were the seats we wanted," she continued. The woman was plain with reddish, curly hair, and her voice had the most obnoxious pitch.

"I'm sorry," I replied, "We got here first. My friends and

I want to be together."

"If you wanted to be together, why didn't you stay at home?" she mimicked my voice.

"We wanted to be together at the communal baths," Bridget replied, her pleasant smile on.

The woman's sulky expression showed that she was not satisfied with Bridget's polite answer, but she did not say anything else. Her group chose seats on the bench in front of ours; these were less desirable because other women would be pacing back and forth through the doors leading inside. She literally threw her bag at the bench.

Bridget remarked, "The Russian soul is so passionate, isn't it?" Rose and I smiled—different smiles. Rose started to undress, beatific, no words spoken. I said, "It's getting hot and we haven't even gone inside."

Undressing, I looked around at the grandiose Beaux Arts building. It had decayed with the passing of years, but the pre-revolutionary grandeur was still visible due to the spaciousness, the hardwood frames, and the faded stained-glass windowpanes. The room was busy, noisy. For the most part, the Sandunov Baths had a distinguished clientele. Some women unpacked sponges of various qualities and sizes, soap bars of different colors and shapes, foreign shampoos—a real luxury.

As the women took off their clothes, their body odors filled the air. I smelled acidic vinegar, like spoiled white wine. Could dead mice, even skunks, be lying around unnoticed?

I took time to look over the women's naked bodies. The older women seemed larger than life, fleshy, overweight, fat drooping down their bellies. A few young women, blond, skin fair as pearls, had their pubic hair trimmed short. What a professional job! The woman with the reddish, curly hair, who had addressed me earlier had heavy stretch marks.

Soon we were all ready to go inside. Modesty seemed unnecessary, bare bodies passed each other now as if clothed. We needed to place a scarf over our hair, a bathhouse rule. Pretty women tied the scarves stylishly, making a fashion statement.

Naked, each of us was eager to enter our first-choice space. As the women rushed to their preferred parlors, they stumbled over each other again.

"Rose, I want you to decide where we're going first," Bridget said.

"Laura, what do you think?" Rose said, turning to me. "Maybe we should take a shower. We need to, anyway, it's the rule."

"Fine with me," I replied with the CLO job in mind, eager to appear accommodating to Bridget.

We crammed into the small space. The water came at us from all sides, not only from the ceiling. Pipes ran around the shower walls bringing the water through small holes. I felt tickled all over, as if men were squeezing my body with a dozen hands. The women next door were roaring with laughter. They ran the water very hot, then very cold, and our shower was affected as well. Once in a while they turned the water so hot that one of us stepped out, only to return a few seconds later.

After the shower we jumped into the cool pool. It was a ten-by-twelve-foot basin, already crowded by the time we got in. There was no space to swim laps, only to exercise in tiny spots. As we giggled, an energetic blonde addressed us, "It's not common to hear English here. Obviously you don't know what you're doing. You are just fooling around. Let me show you," she bossed.

Managing to get the two of us close to the edge of the pool, she started to exercise. "*Raz, dva,*" she counted with zest. Her back against the wall, she pushed her knees to her face; right knee first, left one next. When she finished, she started with both knees at the same time. "Lean against the wall. You'll get stronger, follow me," she commanded.

"I'm going along just to please the blond woman," I said to Bridget, again trying to ingratiate myself.

"Nice of you, Laura. The woman enjoys teaching us," she answered.

Rose was not ready to follow anybody's instructions that morning. After a couple of exercises she left for the middle of the basin, but Bridget and I obeyed the orders. "*Raz, dva, tri*," one, two, three, our commander continued. We went along, dutifully.

I noticed that the woman who had wanted our seats on the bench was watching us. Somehow, she did not seem to be having fun; her defiant gaze was remarkable. We did the exercises several times but, after a while, Bridget and I decided to take a break. The woman was too intense.

We wanted to go to the *parnaya*, the Russian euphemism for the extremely hot sauna. We left the pool and queued outside the low entrance.

"This is Russia for you," I said. "Even for the *parnaya* we have to wait in line."

"Laura, this is the only opportunity for these women to clean themselves for a whole week," Bridget answered. "Have you already forgotten that rotten pickled cucumber scent in the dressing room?"

"It's true," Rose agreed, placid.

The CLO job always in mind, I turned to Bridget, expressive, "Yes, I still remember. It's just that I'm not used to so many lines."

We waited with the other women, our bodies pressing against each other. I did not enjoy the closeness, but if I distanced myself from the woman ahead of me, someone else pushed into the line. The delay was long, shortened only when someone left the *parnaya*. Many women had birch branches. When I got inside, I saw them beating—carnally, furiously—their backs, bellies, and legs. It was certainly most invigorating but I wondered if the pain was not greater than the pleasure. Indulgently, they also brought in colorful jars of honey that they spread on face and body alike.

Sweating profusely, the three of us returned to the changing room to rest a bit. As I opened the tea thermos, Rose said with a heartfelt look, "I have to tell you something, I had a dream last night. My baby daughter was exactly like the picture the orphanage sent. When I met her, she stretched her arms towards me. It was so beautiful!"

"That's a premonition, Rose. I bet your meeting is going to be just like that," Bridget said reassuringly.

"Have you and Brian decided on a name?" I asked.

"We've several possibilities, but we want to wait until we meet our daughter."

"A sensible idea. Babies have personalities," Bridget said, again so wisely.

I looked at Rose feeling jealous. She was finally getting what she wanted, the real thing, a baby. Keith and I had been trying for a child, but still without success; maybe the stressful conditions of our life were the cause.

We sipped our tea and talked. Rose was concerned about the return trip, the cold, the baby's adjustment to her new family. After a while, Rose was ready to go back inside and Bridget followed her. I told them I would join them in a few minutes.

I sat at first, but then lay down on the bench. Every single pore of my body exulted. My skin was as soft as velvet. A feeling of deep relaxation came over me. Closing my eyes, I inhaled deeply. The contrast between the cool basin and the *parnaya* was unique. Daydreaming came easily.

Not long after, with eyes still closed, I heard a coarse voice, "You need to move. You cannot lie down here, it takes up too much space."

"Who said?" I asked as I sat up, annoyed to be interrupted. I recognized the woman who had wanted our bench.

As I rose, her stretch marks seemed like scars. "My friends and I have had this bench since we arrived. I'm lying down because they're inside. I'm not taking anyone else's space."

"I moved my clothes to this bench," she said indicating the left side, where my feet had been. "You're dirtying them."

"How can that be? I just returned from the *parnaya*. Besides, I was not even touching them," I answered.

"Oh, yes, you were," she continued. A couple of women on the bench nearby, hearing the exchange, looked at us.

It seemed best to ignore my opponent, so I tried to lie down again. As I turned, the woman said, "I can see you want to give me trouble." She pushed me aside. "You cannot lie here," she insisted in a shrill voice.

"I'm not touching your clothing, I never did," I told her.

"Yes, you did."

"No, I didn't."

"You're disturbing me," the woman said harshly.

"Tough," I replied, enraged. And something crossed my mind, I don't know what. It was, maybe, the primal atmosphere around me. But, hoping my foe would leave me alone, I gave her the finger.

The woman's expression changed more than I wanted.

"You insulted me, I'm going to report you to the *dezhurnaya*." As she said this, she turned her back on me and walked towards the door determined to find the supervisor on duty.

Following her with my eyes, I saw Bridget and Rose coming in. This is getting nasty, I thought. The baths are always crowded, my assailant must hate foreigners who take the space of Soviet women at the baths. But had Bridget seen my gesture? I was not sure. If she had, she would be horrified. More to the point, it would end my chances of getting the CLO job. Surely, Bridget would not want to leave her position in the hands of a "hot-head."

As they came closer, Bridget had a concerned expression. "Laura, what on earth is going on?" she asked in a soothing voice. Her tone upset me further.

"That woman annoyed me, so I annoyed her back," I said.

"What did she say?"

"She went to call the bath's attendant."

"Oh, Laura, we don't need this."

"Sorry, Bridget, but this is what we're getting," I said, wishing the crisis would end quickly. Many threats were never carried out in Russia.

We did not have to wait long; soon after, my adversary returned, accompanied by a woman wearing a white gown. I had no time to dress, and Bridget had come in at the worst possible moment. I started to feel defenseless. It was not every day that I exposed my body in front of strangers.

Rose, happy in her own world, took a bottle of shampoo from her bag and went back inside.

Bridget stayed around, I did not know why. Did she feel she needed to be of assistance? Her CLO position demanded, after all, that she help people understand the labyrinths of this country. Or was she simply nosy—and eager to see what would happen?

I did not care to ask.

The *dezhurnaya*—an old woman, tall and serious— stood amidst the nude bodies in her white gown. Politely, she addressed me, "I've heard many complaints throughout the years, but nothing like this. This *tovarishch*," this comrade, she said, pointing to the woman with the stretch marks, "says you, a foreigner, gave her the finger. Is that true?"

I used my standard phrase when in trouble in Moscow, I said that I did not understand her, that I could not speak Russian. By now a circle of curious women surrounded us, watching what was going on. The *dezhurnaya* repeated the question, but was getting nowhere, since I did not reply. My foe told her that I spoke Russian, that I knew what she was asking.

Bridget interrupted, baffled, "What is the supervisor asking, Laura? I couldn't understand a couple of her phrases."

"I don't know."

"How come? Can you explain what's going on?" her voice sounded concerned again.

By that time I had enough of Bridget, too. "I don't know what she's talking about, alright?" I said, trying to get her off my back.

Bridget looked hurt.

Now the only thing I wanted was to get dressed, so I took down the hanger and removed my clothing. But the boss was not about to let me go.

"Did you make an improper gesture—or not?" she asked again.

I did not reply, but realized that Bridget looked bewildered. My antagonist and the *dezhurnaya* talked to each other now. The women who gathered around started taking sides. Bridget realized that it was better to keep her mouth shut, and I was grateful for that.

My rival argued with the *dezhurnaya*, she wanted her to do something, though I did not understand exactly what. A pretty devushka, a young girl in a psychedelic scarf— maybe she felt good about herself—said that the *tovarishch* wanted to fight with me for no reason. Another woman said that I was lying on the bench, and that we were not allowed to do that. Amidst a chorus of voices, I stopped paying attention to the conversation. At least I was already partially dressed.

Assailant and supervisor got at each other's throats. After a while, I realized the troublemaker wanted an apology. Since I had decided that I would not speak any Russian, I could not apologize. I continued dressing.

After a pause, the *dezhurnaya* addressed me straightforwardly, "We don't like hooligans in this country. And this is how you behaved. You broke the rules, you must leave the baths."

I continued dressing, as if I had not heard what she said.

She turned to Bridget now, hoping to find a sympathetic ear, "Are you with an embassy?" she asked.

"Yes, we are," Bridget replied bravely, a smile on her face.

"Which one?"

"The American Embassy," Bridget replied. With the Cold War going on, it did not cross Bridget's mind to mention another embassy as a stratagem to contain the discussion; any other embassy would have been better.

The *dezhurnaya* turned to me again, "Show me your *diplomaticheskaya kartochka*," she commanded. Indeed my name and embassy affiliation were printed on the diplomatic card.

I shrugged my shoulders, as if I did not understand her again. I was not even sure I had brought my diplomatic identification, as I had changed my regular purse that morning.

"Please leave as soon as you can," the *dezhurnaya* finally ordered. "This is the best I can do for you."

Boots already on, I said to Bridget, "You and Rose stay here. I'm getting out. I'll wait for you in the car. Don't rush, I'll be fine."

The bitch looked on, a victorious expression on her ugly face. "What do I care?" I thought. "The supervisor doesn't have my identification, I can always return to the Sandunov Baths."

I picked up my bag, pushed through the circle of human flesh—the room's smell was unbearable now—and made my way to the door. In the car, I paged through *Time Magazine* while trying to keep warm.

When Bridget and Rose arrived at the car, Rose said, "Laura, you should have seen how Bridget handled the *dezhurnaya*. When I came back, she was still going on and on, but Bridget got rid of her real fast."

"It's my job, after all, to see that things run smoothly," Bridget said. And, turning my way, she added, "All's well, that ends well. Don't you agree, Laura?"

I only moaned a yes.

Bridget left Moscow without my ever knowing whether she realized what had happened that morning. I did not ask her for a reference, and when the time came, I did not submit an application for the CLO job either. Despite Bridget's best smile, I suspected that I would not be selected.

On the Trail of Tolstoy

To celebrate our impending anniversary, Keith and I wanted to visit Tolstoy's country estate at Yasnaya Polyana, Clear Field, located more than two hundred kilometers south of Moscow. Since both of us admired the great writer, the trip was a good occasion to share a common interest and spend a couple of days together. When I suggested the outing, Keith could not have been more pleased.

Tolstoy was born at Yasnaya Polyana and lived there more than half a century. It was at the estate that he produced masterpieces such as *Anna Karenina* and *War and Peace*. He cherished this land, acknowledging its influence both on his writing and on his character. During the winter the snow enticed him; in his diary entries, Tolstoy described the power of snowstorms to nurture his soul.

Like a pilgrim, I wanted to honor the source of the author's inspiration, look around with my own eyes. The journey was a way to share Tolstoy's appreciation of the countryside; and, also, a tribute to the landscape that filled him with joy. The birch trees, the old, splendid apple orchard, the meadow close to his study window all seemed within reach. I felt a longing for the oak and the lime forest of which I had only seen pictures.

It was already October, a trip to the estate any later in the year with snow on the ground was out of the question.

Since the Soviet government required that Keith and I

get special permission to travel outside of Moscow, I went to the American Embassy's Miscellaneous Services department to make the arrangements. These "mysterious services," as they were often called by the Americans, were handled by UPDK, the office in the Soviet Foreign Ministry in charge of all services for the diplomatic corps. The purpose of the UPDK embassy branch was to facilitate the coexistence between the Americans and the Soviets.

As I entered the large room filled with desks, a young Soviet employee stood by her chair. She was a brunette in late pregnancy, barely nineteen years old, with a pretty face. Her lovely light brown eyes shone with infinite boredom. Somehow, a hint of conceit in the shape of her mouth showed that she did not welcome my presence, I immediately sensed impending trouble. Laura, I heard myself utter, give this woman a chance.

I addressed the young secretary as politely as I could, "Good morning! How are you?" I paused; there was no reply. "Our car needs a spare part that will only arrive from Finland in two or three weeks. But our anniversary is coming up, and my husband and I would like to rent a car to go to Yasnaya Polyana the weekend after next. Also, we would like to book a hotel in Tula for one night."

The woman stared at me and replied, "Your plans might be difficult to fulfill; with a driver, the trip is going to be costly."

"Oh, I'm sorry, I didn't make myself clear," I answered back. "We don't need a driver, both my husband and I have drivers' licenses. We only need a car."

"I can't arrange that," she pronounced sternly. "At the moment, all the cars for you—I mean you people affiliated with the American Embassy—come with a driver."

"Why is that, may I ask?"

"This is the way we run things in our country."

"Would you do me a favor, please?" I insisted. "Would

you call your boss and explain that we'd like to rent a car without a driver?"

The secretary's eyes turned to the phone on her desk; she sat down and I saw her dialing a number. I also heard her request clearly, she did repeat what I had asked. When the answer came, she placed the gray, old-fashioned receiver back in the stand. She turned to me, her patience seemed endless now.

"Sorry, but it's the way I told you. Also, my supervisor passed on the message that there aren't any cars available for the weekend after next."

"Why?"

"I don't know, that's what he told me," the secretary added.

"Maybe you could call the Intourist travel agency. Since they are a governmental office, they might help!" I tried to sound positive.

"They can't help you. Intourist only goes to Yasnaya Polyana during the week, never on weekends."

The woman must have noticed that I was about to get angry, because she suggested, "Why don't you talk to my colleague over here? My associate might be able to help you with the hotel reservations."

It was unclear why I was supposed to make hotel reservations if Keith and I could not get a car; it seemed the woman was trying to get rid of me. But leaving rationality aside, I addressed the other clerk who had overheard our conversation. I repeated my wish to reserve a night in a hotel in Tula.

"I must tell you upfront, to book a hotel in Tula might be as difficult as renting a car. The booking will cost you six rubles, and, if you cancel, you have to pay another six rubles."

I felt as if floating in outer space—the sensation was common in Moscow—but I only replied with conviction,

"With permission to travel, my husband and I don't intend to cancel the reservation."

She stared at me; I decided to turn to the pregnant brunette again.

"You haven't told me yet how much it costs to rent a car, with a driver, for the weekend."

The secretary used the phone and then turned to me again. "My supervisor tells me that you need not only a car and a driver but a guide as well."

"What?" I asked louder than I intended.

"You don't need to get upset," the brunette said coolly.

"Can you answer my question: how much will the trip cost?" I was trying hard to keep my composure.

"Something like one hundred and twenty rubles a day. And we have a rule: you need to pay either in dollars or in Deutch Marks." She continued matter-of-factly, "You can go now to my other colleague, that one over there, at the far corner. She is the person in charge of filling out forms." She pointed at the clerk. "You need a form asking authorization to travel. If the Ministry of Foreign Affairs grants it, we'll let you know. Good-bye for now."

That evening Keith and I discussed the situation, and we never filled out the form. Keith saw my disappointment but from the way the conversation had gone, he suspected that our outing would not be allowed. Tolstoy would have to wait for our visit; the weekend of our anniversary we flew to London.

Annoyed with the Soviet system, I complained the following day to Evgenya, my Russian teacher at the embassy. I wanted to chat, her interest in Russian grammar was too extreme.

I loved Evgenya, she was such a great teacher that I even forgave her for smelling of disinfectant, not soap. Evgenya was a true believer in the Soviet system, there seemed to be no irony, no double thinking. An American friend, also a student of hers, had mentioned that Evgenya might be a KGB colonel in disguise. What do I care, I thought, as long as I refrain from discussing personal matters with her? It fascinated me to see someone with that level of certainty, so very few misgivings. In the West, only religious fanatics had that kind of conviction. She knew white, black, and very few, if any, shades of gray in between.

When Evgenya heard my complaint, she answered with her usual socialistic fervor that the country had rules, rules with which my husband and I needed to comply.

It just happened that when I crossed the Kremlin that day to attend my lesson at the American Embassy, I had seen a demonstration, just a few dozen people with placards praising the government. I had read one of them, "With enthusiasm, we salute our beloved communist leaders."

I continued with Evgenya, "This is bizarre: I passed the Kremlin on my way here and, as usual, I saw a pro-government demonstration."

"Laura, what's so surprising about that? In this country we respect our superiors," Evgenya exclaimed.

"We respect governments in the West, too, particularly if they deserve it. But we protest when there are abuses of power."

"That doesn't happen here, our leaders know how to watch out for us. They help us, they protect us; in turn, we're thankful."

"They protect you so thoroughly?" I felt like provoking Evgenya just a bit. "Gosh, aren't you scared?"

"Scared of what?"

"Did you ever read George Orwell? Have you ever heard that absolute power can corrupt absolutely?"

"Who is George Orwell?"

"He is a British writer. I think you'd enjoy reading him, he might broaden your horizons. "

"Don't you know that I don't speak—or read—any English? Russian and its grammar are enough for me."

I smiled. In my mind Evgenya was afraid of speaking English. She had plenty of opportunities to learn it with her American students, she had been a teacher for over fifteen years. For me, Evgenya suspected that if she made an effort to speak or read English, her fanatical world would crumble in a few minutes.

But Evgenya was smart, and she was determined to save the day. She asked if I would like to read in class one of Tolstoy's short stories; she suggested *Master and Man*. Keith had the book in our library at home, so I promised to bring it to class the following day. My time had not been wasted. And when we started reading the story, my attraction to the famous Russian author only deepened.

A few weeks later—with me still complaining about the aborted visit to Yasnaya Polyana between pages of *Master and Man*—Evgenya offered another solution. She suggested a further step in my knowledge of the writer, this time a visit to the Tolstoy literary museum in Moscow, located at Prechistenka Street, No. 11. She mentioned that Tolstoy's complete works were there. Also, that the house was filled with manuscripts, first editions, notes, personal letters, photographs, and even Tolstoy's drawings.

I thanked Evgenya for her new plan. And so, one afternoon after class, I headed over to visit the museum.

Evgenya had not warned me, but it was obvious that the Soviets had adopted Tolstoy as their own writer. The museum was completely structured ideologically, with every word, every detail, politically correct according to Soviet doctrine. At the entrance to each room were small wall labels, both in Russian and English, describing the room's contents. The first room set the tone for the frame of mind to follow—it laid out the Bolshevik assessment of Tolstoy's work. The room displayed not only a huge Bolshevik flag but also several original editions of the newspaper *Pravda*—

Truth in English—praising the author soon after the Revolution. I read the title of the nearest wall label, "Lenin on Tolstoy" which dealt, appropriately, with Lenin's judgment of the author. It read in Russian, "Lenin wrote seven articles on Tolstoy, who was his favorite author...," and continued later on, "Tolstoy, as a mirror of the Russian Revolution, stated that...." The Russian and the English versions of the framed descriptions were very different. Lenin's reviews had been omitted in the English versions.

After a tour of all the rooms I was unable to distinguish between historical fact and communist dogma, but I left the museum, nevertheless, with the feeling of a well-spent afternoon. A touching detail in one of the rooms stayed with me: the original illustrations made in crayon, in 1898-99, by L. O. Pasternak—the father of the Russian poet and novelist Boris Pasternak—for Tolstoy's novel, *Resurrection.*

Following the visit, I told Evgenya how instructive the museum had been. Pleased with my devotion to Tolstoy, Evgenya gave me yet another idea. She recommended, this time, that I visit Tolstoy's house in Moscow, after all he had lived there for over fifteen years. The house was located in a street that bore the writer's name, and which the Soviets had turned into a museum as early as 1921.

We had been reading *Master and Man* at a fast pace once a week and were close to the end. I told Evgenya that I wanted to visit Tolstoy's house only under heavy snowfall; she answered that I would not have long to wait, the depths of winter were drawing close.

One day in early January, I watched snowflakes filling the streets, inch by inch, from the crack of dawn. By early afternoon, the atmosphere seemed most conducive for my much delayed meeting with Tolstoy's domestic surroundings. I quickly consulted a map of the city and found the location of the house. Soon after, I got into the car and drove carefully through a Moscow blizzard in full power. The streets had not been plowed yet and the car zigzagged as if on skates. The wind was strong, pulling the car left and right as I went along.

Tolstoy's wooden mansion emerged on a quiet side street off a major intersection on the Sadovoye Koltso. I parked by the garden's low fence, there was not a soul in sight on the street. A small plaque by the main entrance indicated my arrival at Tolstoy's home. The house was brown with green shutters, surrounded by a few birch trees, and exuded a peaceful feeling of rustic simplicity.

It was virtually dark in the entrance hall. The attendant at the front door took my fur coat and sold me a ticket. She asked me to leave my backpack with her. Since a book was a permanent companion on my expeditions in Moscow, *Master and Man* was sticking out of one pocket. Another woman had arrived a few minutes earlier, a bureaucratic type; she was very slim and tall, with very short hair, and she wore a two-piece dark gray suit. With a beam in her eyes she noticed my book and soon withdrew to a nearby corridor.

"I really wanted to come here today," I told the attendant while paying for the ticket.

"It's getting late," she answered.

"I know, but I wanted to see Tolstoy's house in the middle of a storm."

"You chose the right day. The house is nearly empty, it's all yours." She continued in an officious manner, "Today is grounds inspection day, the clerk you just saw—the woman who went inside—is our government superintendent."

"She did look like an inspector!" I said half-amused.

"Hurry up," she continued seriously, not seeming to enjoy my remark. "Soon you won't be able to see anything—the house doesn't have electricity."

"Is that so?" I was surprised.

"As much as possible, we try to keep the house as it was in Tolstoy's time. Let the snow's light be your guide."

"How's that possible?"

"You'll see, the snow outside throws light into the rooms inside."

"I didn't know that!"

"You know now." The woman hurried me on while gesticulating with her arms, "Hush, hush, don't lose time talking, during the winter we close early, at 3:00."

I started to walk around slowly, meeting Tolstoy at one of his houses had taken quite a long time. I passed through the old-fashioned kitchen; then the dinning room, where the British china that the family used every day was on display. It was as if the family was about to return for the evening meal. The children's playroom, near the kitchen, had a child's colorful wooden horse and a doll's sled. The rooms were all packed with furniture and various objects; they were cozy, warm, and radiated intimacy.

The public part of the house was located upstairs and I climbed the stairway after admiring a few more details downstairs. On display was a huge, embalmed bear's head that Tolstoy had hunted himself before his religious conversion; and Tolstoy's bicycle, a present from the Moscow Society of Velocipede Lovers that, according to the wall label, the author had learned to ride at age sixty-seven.

The renowned ballroom was located on the second floor. Snow swirled around the windows, heavier than ever before that day. A grand piano stood at one end of the room. The furniture was refined, the sofas covered with red brocade; oriental rugs, silver, vases, lace, and many other delicate ornaments decorated the large room. Many pictures of family members accompanied by writers and artists were on display. Copies of originals at Yasnaya Polyana of Ilya Repin's family portraits were on the walls.

The attendant in the ballroom noticed how attentively I studied the decoration. She said, "It'll be dark soon. Why did you arrive so late?"

"It was my dream to visit the house in a snowstorm; I didn't know there was no electricity here," I answered.

"You studied every object in detail, as if you were a detective."

"The decor is so superb! Also, I must confess, I have a fascination for interiors."

"It's Count Tolstoy's house, after all," she said, pride filling her voice.

"The house is grand, but not opulent, not ostentatious," I added.

"Like all great men, Tolstoy liked to live simply," she replied.

"Still, there's an aristocratic feeling here. The house is simple and elegant at the same time."

"It was Tolstoy's wife, Countess Sophia Andreyevna, who wanted it that way. If Tolstoy had lived here alone, the house would have been even simpler."

The living room was next door. The attendant there was talking softly to the superintendent, as if they were in a sanctuary. The inspector turned in my direction and sized me up.

Again, I observed the room meticulously, taking my time. I noticed the old-fashioned clock, the mirrors framed by elaborate carved wood, the corners filled with stylish round tables; the candelabra, the small, decorated boxes, and the statuettes. It was getting darker with each step I took, and indeed, as the entrance attendant had mentioned, it was the snow's brightness entering the windows that illuminated the room. A peculiar shade upon the objects multiplied them by now, as if they were not one, but many; they appeared dim, mysterious, enigmatic. It was as if the furnishings were wrapped up in the most voluptuous of shadows.

Now I wanted to see Tolstoy's studio and asked the attendant for directions. She said, "Our writer liked to work far from the noises of the house; he had many children, also many servants. Go through that corridor, over there," she indicated the far end of the house with her chin. "You'll find it at the end of the narrow hallway, on the right."

The superintendent realized that I was a foreigner when I asked the question. With a half smile, she started up a conversation, "You seem to enjoy our revered Lev Nikolayevich." In the Russian fashion, she used Tolstoy's first name and patronymic.

"Oh, I love him! For a long time I've wanted to come here."

"At the entrance, I noticed that you're reading a favorite story of ours, *Master and Man*. Good, isn't it?"

"The description of the blizzard is one of the best things I've read in my life. This is why I decided to come here today, with a snowstorm at its heights."

"There's nothing special about the storm in the story; in this country we have blizzards all the time," she continued with a disdainful smile. "What's special is how the master, Brekhunov, dies to save Nikita, his servant," she concluded.

I was having too good a time to debate the inspector. A bit of humor would have come in handy, but I felt too awed by Tolstoy's surroundings. So I asked instead, while returning the inspector's half smile, "Well, isn't that a matter of interpretation?"

"You foreigners don't understand us." The inspector's eyes were now as overcast as her dark gray suit. "Brekhunov made his money taking advantage of others, he was a merchant all his life. But, at the verge of death, he saw how empty his life had been. This is why Tolstoy wrote the story: to remind us that he, himself, discovered the emptiness of his wealth later in life."

I imagined that the inspector was a Slavophile, filled with the official truth, those people did not welcome foreigners. Feeling provocative, I added like a dissident, "Maybe what Brekhunov did can be seen as the most Christian of virtues, charity."

"Nonsense!" My words were an heresy to the official's ear.

"Let's reason together," I tried to keep the dialogue going. "Tolstoy had already gone through his religious conversion when he wrote the story. Isn't it possible that he's describing a virtue of Christian life, 'Help thy neighbor'? "

"Outsiders always feel entitled to an opinion!" The inspector continued in the same tone, "I'm telling you: Brekhunov decided to save his servant, Nikita, because he felt the peasant's life was worth more than his own. This is why he used his body to cover Nikita's. He knew that only one of them, not both, had a chance to survive the blizzard."

"I know that. But don't you think his gesture can have more than one meaning?"

"No, the gesture has only one meaning." The inspector's pitch rose, I feared Tolstoy's house might come down with its thunder. "At the time, our Lev Nikolayevich had already developed a strong class consciousness, he was already an early socialist. He had Brekhunov save Nikita as his ultimate moment of truth. The great Tolstoy revered his own country roots, the peasantry. Above all, he was an admirer of 'natural man.' And Nikita, the peasant, epitomized all that."

"What about Tolstoy's Christian conversion later in life?"

"You need guidance." The inspector did not answer my question. "It's not here in Moscow, but only at Yasnaya Polyana, the place where the writer was born, that you can see—really see—what I'm talking about. You should visit the estate one day."

"Believe me, I've tried," I uttered ironically, waving a

quick good-bye.

I turned around and followed the attendant's directions to the far end of the house. And, there, at the end of the narrow corridor, was Tolstoy's studio. *Resurrection*, a work of fiction dealing with spiritual regeneration, had been written here. The room was small and sober, the furniture sparse. To the right stood the wooden desk where the writer worked. Opposite were a couple of armchairs; the rug on the floor had seen better days. The heavy snow falling against the tiny window directly across from the door illuminated the room. Tolstoy's desk was enveloped by the most seductive of twilights.

When I left the house a few minutes later, the snow seemed about to wipe out the city of Moscow. I drove back home slowly, my car still skating through the streets. Once, I had to pull over because the wind was so strong. The stop gave me a chance to pull *Master and Man* from my backpack and find the passage I wanted. It was an old verse by Pushkin that Petrukha, one of the peasants, had evoked when Brekhunov and Nikita stopped at his grandfather's house to get warm along the way. It read:

> The storm be darkling over the sky,
> It spins the whirling snow,
> Now like a beast it roars out wild,
> Now like a babe sobs low.

I felt gratified that Tolstoy's spirit—in the voice of a peasant reciting Russian poetry— had prevailed in my mind well above the inspector's words.

Keith and I shared a moment of togetherness over dinner that evening, engaging in one of those literary discussions we so much enjoyed. I told him yet again about the alluring power of nature; how enchanted I had been by the snow spinning against the windows, the shadow cast over the objects in the grand rooms upstairs, the twilight on Tolstoy's desk. Keith suggested we visit the house together.

After dinner, with the help of a dictionary, I finished *Master and Man* in a single stretch.

The Puppetmaster

I was beside myself the day that Keith and I went to see Obraztsov, the famous Russian puppeteer. The previous afternoon my upstairs neighbor, Ruth, had told me that while her family was dining out, the KGB had entered her apartment and cut the plastic handles of her baby's portable crib. When I shared the ominous story with Keith that evening, his response was that I knew the country we were living in, and that I needed to be stronger. Longing for a word of understanding that his stoic diplomatic veneer did not allow him to share, I felt dismissed.

The chance to see Obraztsov came as a great relief. Since Soviet TV was filming for a worldwide audience, the show promised to be unique. Jim Henson, the American puppeteer, would also be there in person and he was scheduled to perform at the ambassador's residence the following day. Keith had been working with the embassy team to set up both performances and had been rewarded with two complimentary tickets.

To give my spirits a lift, I dressed up for the occasion in a low-cut, dark-red, silk dress, with black suede shoes and a small matching handbag. I put on my favorite earrings, sapphires encrusted with diamonds, a wedding gift from my mother-in-law. Ready much earlier than necessary, I was sipping tea in the living room when the phone rang. It was Keith.

"Laura, I'm sorry, I'm late. Lots of small things came up at the last minute. But I'll pick you up in half an hour."

"This is the third time you are late this week. Why don't you ask someone else to take over?"

"I can't, David asked me to stay."

"I bet David is on his way to the theater with Mary this very minute."

"Dear, please, you understand the way things are. I won't be long."

"The way things are can be changed. This applies to work, marriage, and life," I barely said before Keith hung up.

When Keith finally arrived home we drove hastily through Gorky Street to reach the Moscow outer Ring Road. The rush hour traffic was heavy, but Keith managed the best he could. Already in Sadovaya-Samotyochnaya, we surfed among dirty lorries and overcrowded, slow-moving Ladas. As soon as we saw the theater—with hardly enough time to admire its splendid iron clock—Keith said, "Go in and sit down. I'll be there in a minute."

I stepped into the entrance hall. At the end, the small auditorium was fully packed, but the house lights were still on as the attendant hurried me to my seat. Along the aisle, I waved to several embassy couples in the audience. An irrepressible wave of self-pity came over me when I realized I was the only spouse with an empty seat at her side.

The curtain went up to thunderous applause as Obraztsov stepped on stage; the show was about to start with Keith nowhere to be seen. I looked over my shoulder a couple of times but could not find him. Soon, Obraztsov took over the stage, the audience, and me.

The first sketch was a puppet's version of *Carmen*, the Bizet opera. Behind a screen, the puppeteer brought the characters to life using only his hands. No strings. Outfitted in huge costumes, the hands had a life of their own. Now they dressed as the gypsy, the jilted brigadier, the bullfighter. The lovers were fighting and *Carmen*, the main character, was going to pay for her mistakes with her life.

I watched, enraptured. And filled with emotion I sympathized with *Carmen* and her follies. Aware of Keith's absence my mind wandered off. What price would I pay if my marriage had been a mistake?

Suddenly, I started to sob uncontrollably. My contact lens floated wildly on tears that I tried to wipe off with my hands; but, with no kleenex available, the tears poured down my face. I managed to cry silently but feared that people noticed my state of mind.

I hurried out of the auditorium just before the intermission started, while people were still applauding passionately. Keith was standing at the closest exit door. "The attendant wouldn't let me in, but I saw most of the performance," he said.

"I need to go to the bathroom, I've been crying like crazy."

"Really? It doesn't show."

Once in the bathroom I rushed to the mirror. Its surface must have been flawless long ago, but it was now blemished with countless black spots. A diagonal fracture was fused together with tape. I saw two red eyes, as red as a bullfighter's cape. Black mascara circled them, as if I had been beaten by a violent husband. There was no toilet paper, no paper towels. Hastily, I tried to grab an old, dirty towel, but it was attached to a metal bar too far from the sink. So, I had to curve my hand like a shell, scoop up water from the tap and try to wash the mascara away. As the mirror stood behind me, also far from the sink, I could not see what I was doing.

When I returned to the foyer, I was on fire. Keith was alone, pacing back and forth, avoiding people.

"You jerk," I burst out. "You told me it didn't show that I had been crying. But in the mirror I looked like you had beaten the hell out of me. Why did you lie?"

"I didn't see anything."

"You are a joke!"

"Laura, please, let's not argue here."

"That's fine," I said, waving at a few embassy acquaintances moving around the foyer. We paced up and down the hall in silence for a few minutes until I asked Keith, "Tell me, what did you think of the performance?"

"Very artistic, fine technique. Obraztsov has been in the business for decades. He's over eighty, you know."

"I don't mean that. I know he's old. What did you think of *Carmen*?"

"She was great."

"Is that all you have to say?"

"What else do you want me to tell you?" Keith whined.

"You have no feelings. You're worse than a puppet," I snapped.

"Why? Because I didn't cry like you?"

"No, not that. You have no heart, you leave me alone all the time."

"No, I don't."

"You know what? I might as well find someone else to talk to. Someone real, someone who listens."

"Go ahead, good luck."

Crossing the foyer, I got in line for a glass of mineral water at the *bufet*. The sight of the fruit juices on display, their dark colors, turned my stomach. Keith paced nearby, pretending he was not watching. If I looked in his direction, he turned away.

David's wife, Mary, was ahead of me in the line talking to someone else. I liked her—she bore her age rather well, was cultured, elegant. She came over after she got her drink, "Hi, Laura, are you enjoying the show?"

"Oh, so very much. The man is outstanding. Keith and I were almost late, but just managed to get here on time."

"Really?" she replied. "I made sure David got home early today."

"I bet you did," I answered with a smile.

As I was approaching the puppets on display in the glass case nearby, the curtain bell rang that intermission was over. Keith's eyes met mine from afar. Without speaking, we fell in step and went inside together.

Obraztsov's next piece was about the law of the jungle. His hands wore the huge costumes of two animals of unequal size, fighting. One hand was dressed as a lion, the other as an eagle. The latter was a fierce animal for its species, but nothing compared to a large mammal. The bird's beak fighting back nonstop was useless. The lion was, unequivocally, superior. Little by little, intently, the lion tore apart the valiant bird, inflicting, at last, the mortal wound.

As we watched, Keith's beeper sounded loud enough for everyone to hear. He got up and told me that if he could not return, I should wait for him at the theater's entrance.

This second piece also received deafening applause at the end. As usual, the Soviets clapped their hands rhythmically, as if following a command; the foreigners attending the show followed suit. Shouts of "bravo," well done, sounded from everywhere. Obraztsov smiled affectionately at the spectators.

The puppeteer slid into an encore when the applause abated. Now his hands were dressed as two drunken friends coming down the street. The scene was surprisingly real. The two men walked slowly, leaning awkwardly into each other, bottles in hand. Still alone, I wished I had Keith's hand to hold on to.

After the show, people got up to leave, but I felt unable to move from my seat. Standing up for the ovation had been easy; I could soon sit down again. But now I needed to leave the theater, follow the crowd. Slowly, I trudged up the aisle, wondering: would Keith be waiting? Would my marriage survive my husband's overbearing career?

As I continued down the aisle, a man smiled at me. He was a middle-aged Russian, with well-groomed, gray hair parted to the side. There was something comforting about his appearance. He said, "I was sitting a few rows behind you and from a certain angle I could see your face throughout the performance. At the end, you seemed somewhere else, maybe in seventh heaven."

"I was in seventh heaven, indeed, wherever that might be. Obraztsov is amazing."

"He's our best puppeteer."

"He truly is in a class of his own."

"In the foyer I heard you speaking English with another woman. What embassy are you with?"

"American."

"I see. You were crying during *Carmen*. You don't look American. Are you Spanish?"

"No, I'm Portuguese."

As we reached the foyer the man said, "I see you're alone, can I invite you for a drink? Let's go downtown, I have my car outside." I liked his gray hair, his warm smile.

"Thank you," I said, my heart lifting at the prospect. "But my husband's waiting for me outside." As much as I wanted a man's attention, I could not possibly accept a stranger's invitation, the man might have been a KGB agent in disguise.

"Some other time, maybe," he replied. "Good-bye for now. Nice talking to you."

I smiled back.

Outside, I looked through the crowd and realized that Keith was not at the entrance. Waiting, I noticed that my small purse was open; I closed it, looking to see if something had dropped, but there were too many people around to search the floor thoroughly. All at once Mary walked in my direction. "Keith is still tied up at the ambassador's residence," she said. "We're giving you a ride." After a pause, she continued warmly, "What took you so long to come out?"

"I was day-dreaming," I replied.

The three of us chatted on the way back. The show had had a captivating effect on them. They were beaming, happy—in the best American manner, all sunshine and apple pie.

"You know, Laura, I met Obrazstov last week," David said, proud as always of his high-powered Soviet contacts. "He told me he started to improvise in front of the mirror at the age of seven."

"Interesting."

"*Carmen* was fantastic. I'm sure the performance touched you in a very special way," Mary said, turning her head towards me.

"In fact, it did. How did you guess?"

"I know you, you're a hot-blooded Iberian woman."

"The whole show was very moving," David went on.

"It was," I replied. But soon I felt silent, distant, giving very little of myself. David and Mary continued to chat in the front seat.

Keith was already home when I opened the front door; he had changed from his dark suit into jeans. "Laura, someone on Henson's staff needed me. They're installing television cameras at the ambassador's residence for tomorrow's show. The electricians got fed up and wanted to leave," he said turning to me, asking for a truce.

"Okay, okay."

"You look so pretty today. Do you want a drink?"

"Good idea. How about some port? Meanwhile, I'll change and heat up dinner."

When I got back to the living room two glasses of port were waiting on the end table. I sat on the couch and felt cozy facing the spacious room. On the other side, the antique dining table looked beautiful. Above it, on the wall, hung two fine prints I had bought in the Rue du Bac in Paris.

The wine relaxed me, and after a few sips I told Keith, "We might as well get drunk like the two people in Obraztsov's encore. We might be friends again, even lovers."

"Great," Keith replied.

Feeling reassured, I opened up. "I feel so low, Keith, you can't imagine. A Russian came up to me in the theater asking if I was Spanish. He said he saw me crying during *Carmen*."

"What else did he say?" Keith asked, maybe jealous, maybe defensive.

"He asked which embassy I was with and ended up inviting me for a drink. He looked mature, with gray hair and a reassuring smile," I paused. "I must tell you, you hide your feelings all the time, as if they didn't exist. And you try to do the same to mine. It's so deadly."

"Come on," Keith said, "I've had a busy month. *Carmen* set you off because I left you alone at the theater." As he spoke, he raised his glass to admire the wine's thick texture.

"There you go again! I tell you how I feel and you deny me my own feelings. How amazing! Your manipulation, like Obraztsov's, is an art form."

"Drink your port. Relax," he said, again tilting the wine inside the glass.

"We live in a foreign country. You work all the time and I feel that I don't matter to you." And taking a deep breath I added, "I liked the Russian man who approached me at the theater. If we were in a different city, I might have accepted his invitation. It would have been an escape from you."

"Why are you saying that now?" Keith asked, rubbing his forehead with his hand.

"It took a stranger to see my tears."

"C'mon." As he said this, Keith came closer and wrapped me in his arms. I liked it, I sensed concern. I curled my leg around his, and tried to open his shirt. "Let's make love," I said. "We'll feel better."

"Maybe after dinner, I'm starving; I only ate breakfast today."

I exploded. "You're always tired or hungry! You know what? I'm going out! Sometimes you seem to care—but you don't care enough." I got up from the sofa, put my coat on, and slammed the front door. As I started down the stairs, I heard our phone ringing.

Out in the street I walked and walked; it was foggy, a bit drizzly, a typical Moscow night when snow might fall. I crossed Red Square, passed the Lenin Library further along, and approached the busy intersection of Kalinin and Chaikovsky Streets. People looked like phantoms in an imaginary tale. I turned south without thinking, heading for Spasopeskovskaya Square, where the American ambassador lived at Spaso House.

The drizzle had picked up but the yellow neoclassical building was clearly visible. The quaint square was virtually deserted with the mist pervading it. For a while I stood there, purposefully looking over the *militsioner*'s booth. All the lights in the mansion's facade were on. Like a beggar, I felt like knocking at the door and asking for assistance.

But in my rush I had forgotten my gloves, hat, and scarf. I decided to return home before I froze. I followed the same route back but saw fewer pedestrians on the streets. In the mist, they looked even more like ghosts, erratically darting here and there. As they passed by, I had the feeling I might see someone I knew. Hands in my pockets trying to keep warm, I scrutinized the occasional face that passed by.

As I approached our building in Bolshaya Ordynka, I saw a man walking through the haze. I thought of the Russian at the theater but discarded as unreal the possibility of seeing him again. The figure was heading my way, so, in due time, I would see his face.

As he came closer I realized that, indeed, it was the man who had approached me in the theater. He was looking me straight in the face, his black overcoat enveloped in white mist. Frightened, I asked in disbelief, "What are you doing here, on my street, at this hour?"

"I came by your house to return your driver's license. It must have fallen out of your purse in the theater. I called the American Embassy, and the telephone operator put me through. I know Keith, your husband."

"This is unbelievable. Did you follow me inside the theater?"

"In a way!"

"I didn't even notice I had lost my driver's license. And in the theater you didn't tell me you knew my husband."

"You didn't ask."

"That's true," I agreed, feeling deceived. The feeling of warmth I had towards this stranger in the theater vanished instantly. I felt as if humans were playing games with each other, like wild animals. In comparison, the puppet show seemed safe now. Who would destroy whom? When? At what cost? Alarmed, I only said, "Altogether this has been quite an evening." And thinking of the fastest way to get rid of the man, I added briskly, "Good-night."

"*Spokoynoy nochi*," he replied, disappearing into the fog. The phrase meant, "Have a peaceful night," but his ironic tone disagreed with his words.

I rushed home and Keith was still up; I asked what he had been doing.

"Andreevich, a contact of mine, dropped by. He found your driver's license at the theater and came by to return it."

"He's the stranger I told you about, I saw him outside a few minutes ago. How come you didn't tell me you knew him?"

"I couldn't imagine I knew the man who talked to you."

"I described him."

"That wasn't enough. I have dozens of contacts in this city," he said with a grimace, and then added with a whimsical sparkle in his eyes, "He's just one more political actor."

"In what way?"

"More ways than you care to know." Visibly tired as he spoke, Keith kissed me good night and left the living room. I turned the lights off. In the dark, only inertia drew me to bed that night.

At the Embassy's Dacha

One late afternoon my upstairs neighbor Ruth called, asking if I wanted to accompany her to the dacha, the embassy's country house. On her last visit, she had taken a few snapshots of a family she had met outside the *produkti* shop, the local grocery store. Having taken the family's address, she now wanted to give them the pictures. I was thrilled to go, it was a great opportunity to escape Moscow for a few days.

The dacha was near Khimki, just outside Moscow's outer Ring Road, heading north. The drive, first by highway and then on small country roads, was fairly easy. At the time, foreigners needed a travel permit from the Soviet Government to go outside the outer Ring. However, if traveling only to the dacha, embassy personnel and their families were exempted from the requirement. The embassy community used the place mostly on weekends. During the week, when Ruth wanted to go, it was entirely ours. The air was fresh there, the food tasted better, and we could relax.

Ruth was an artist, and a good one, too. Something unique set her apart from the other embassy spouses. Instead of feasting on gossip, she worked daily at her craft; as a result, her work reflected her incisive view of the Soviet Union. She had a baby girl barely two years old, called Jane, who was going with us as well.

The atmosphere was magnificent the day we arrived at the dacha's large property. Snow still covered everything that late in March, we were reminded of Christmas. The tops of the huge pine trees were barely visible with white flakes scattered over their branches. The dim northern sunlight enveloped the trees as if in a dream.

The dacha was a small house built of well-polished, light pinewood imported from Finland. It was modest but comfortable. The lightwood, made up of perfectly laid out strips, was superbly finished. The pine had been so meticulously cut that it displayed symmetrically, at designated intervals, its natural, dark, round knots. The black, cast-iron fireplace in the living room added an overall feeling of comfort.

As soon as we unloaded the car and had tea, Ruth suggested that we dress warmly and go for a walk in the nearby fields. We needed our heavy coats, boots, fur hats, scarves, and gloves. Jane would ride on a sled that Ruth had ordered from the L.L. Bean Catalog, as sturdy as only Americans can make them. After sitting Jane on the sled, Ruth covered her snowsuit with a rabbit fur coat. Only her eyes, nose, and mouth were visible.

We made our way along snow-covered country roads into the woods. The fresh air was cold and invigorating, and as the ground was quite flat, it was possible to walk briskly. We saw a few cross-country skiers, enjoying the outdoors like us. *Izbas*, peasant wood cottages, were scattered everywhere. Jane smiled blissfully as Ruth pulled the sled.

When we reached the top of a tiny hill, Ruth stopped and gazed toward the horizon. "Look at the pinnacles of that church, Laura," she said pointing. "Isn't that golden onion dome gorgeous? There's a beautiful cemetery next to the church. Let's go there tomorrow morning." And she added, "I want to visit the family in the evening, after dark. I would hate it if someone following us saw where we went."

"Who would do that, here?" I asked.

"I don't know, maybe Sergei, the dacha's gate keeper. I don't want to put the family in a difficult position with our visit. So let's do something else during the day. I want to show you something special at the cemetery."

I did not ask what she had in mind as I enjoyed the suspense. On the way back to the dacha we stopped at the *produkti* shop for supplies to cook dinner.

Early in the morning the following day, dressed warmly again, the three of us left for the cemetery. Jane was once again on the sled, and we walked on the snow for over an hour. We barely talked, focusing our attention on the gorgeous landscape.

When we arrived at the cemetery's tall iron gate, Ruth said, "Let's walk around a bit. The graves are so different from anything I've seen before."

"They are," I said, looking around. "We've stepped back in time."

"Look at the iron fences hedging the graves. Elaborate, aren't they? I've never seen fences painted with this celestial blue anywhere else."

"Neither have I," I answered.

"Look how the gravestones have either a cross or a red star on top. Isn't it unusual?" Ruth reached out and touching the star on the nearby grave, continued, "Look at the large number of graves dating from the Second World War."

"Let me read some of these names," I said, trying to make sense of the Cyrillic alphabet. I read a few inscriptions aloud, "Anatoly Mikhailovich Komarov"; "Tatyana Fyodorovna Morozova"; "Grigory Semionovich Kupechnik."

"Let's go to that far corner now," Ruth said. "Once I found something very touching there. That's what I wanted to show you."

"What was it?" I asked curiously.

"Wait a minute, you'll see."

We walked about the graves, and it took a while for Ruth to maneuver the sled around the tight corners.

Before long Ruth slowed down, and I knew we had arrived at the spot. The grave nearby had a male name and the two dates were close in time. Above it, a small shrine carved in the stone showed the framed photograph of a young boy. Carefully, Ruth brushed the snow from inside the shrine, revealing a small round dish with candy.

"It's still here," she said, amazed. "The boy's mother must visit quite often. Every time I come, the dish has candy."

"How touching," I said. "How did you find this grave?"

"I was here last May." Ruth looked at me, "I came this way because birds were flying low, and I wondered why. The shrine was pretty visible. The birds were pecking at the candy."

"Amazing."

"In the spring these graves are full of flowers. People in the village take good care of their dead."

"This is so moving."

"That's how I get inspiration for my work—I walk around, I look at things," Ruth continued.

"You're remarkable," I said and touched her arm affectionately.

"Let's go home now. We can rest a bit and eat something."

We had lunch at the dacha, then Jane took a nap while Ruth and I made a fire and sat on the floor in front of it, enjoying the warmth. A pungent scent emanated from the burning logs; the flames hissed and danced.

"Ruth, I admire you," I said, feeling totally at ease. "You really make the most of your stay here. This country comes alive through your eyes."

"Thank you," Ruth said appreciatively; but it was nothing she did not know.

"A walk with you is better than a lecture on the history of painting. I see so much through your eyes."

"I'm glad."

"Your view of this country is deep, and tolerant. The child's shrine was enthralling. If I had been at the cemetery with someone else, I probably would have started complaining about how the Soviets let so many of their people die during the Second World War."

"Did they have a choice?"

"That's not the point. My point is that your view is insightful, and mature."

"I wonder about the meaning of the candy at the shrine. Maybe the mother wants to recall the sweetness of her son's short life."

"You might be right."

"Maybe she keeps the candy there so the birds will circle the grave and keep him company."

"It's possible."

We continued talking for a while. When Jane woke up we played with her. Later, we put more logs on the fire and had a light supper. As evening approached, Ruth said it was time to visit the family.

We dressed again for the cold and went out; it was already completely dark. I must have looked concerned because Ruth said, "Don't worry, Laura. I know where these people live. I've been to the village many times before."

"You didn't tell me exactly how you met this family," I said.

"I was outside the *produkti* store, where we bought our food yesterday, trying to take a picture of the door. I wanted the name on top in Cyrillic. They—the father, mother and two children—waited outside patiently, smiling."

"I see."

"When I finished I took a photo of them as well. I asked for their address and promised to give them the snapshots."

"Do they know you're American?"

"Yes. Scott was with me. We told them we were staying at the embassy dacha. They live here, they're used to seeing embassy people come and go."

"Do they speak any English?"

"No. We have to speak Russian."

We headed towards the village with Jane again on the sled. Small streetlights dimly lit the way. Dogs barked here and there as we passed the *izbas*. It was humid, foggy. We had to walk carefully in the snow, watching where we put our feet.

When we reached the family's street, it took a while to find the miniature numbers on the houses, but we managed. At No. 22, unable to find a bell, Ruth knocked forcefully on the door. She took off her dark brown *shapka*, so that the family member who opened the door would recognize her.

A robust man appeared, wearing a red pullover with long sleeves. His blond hair was totally disheveled, he was not expecting company. Remembering Ruth instantly, he greeted her smiling and shouted to his wife.

"Lydia, we have visitors. Look who's here."

"Who is it, Igor?"

"Come see for yourself."

Lydia appeared, flanked by her two children. Like her husband, she must have been in her thirties. She wore a flowery scarf wrapped around her neck, and was healthy looking with a rosy complexion. Her lips were thick, shaped like a heart.

"Come in, come in," she said, greeting us warmly. She turned to Ruth, "It's been a while since we last saw you."

"Yes, but I returned, as promised, and I brought a friend." Ruth introduced me, "This is Laura."

"*Ochen priyatno*," Lydia said, obviously thrilled to have us in her izba, "It is a pleasure to meet you."

Ruth lifted Jane out of the sled and Igor stood it against the outside wall.

We went in and Lydia and Igor helped us out of our coats. The place smelled damp. Lydia invited us to sit at a round table in the living area. Then she lifted one corner of a dark pink drapery covering the table's brazier to stir its glowing coals.

The ceiling was so low that her husband, tall as he was, could hardly stand straight. But the room had a cozy feeling, and was warm. We were not in poor company. The furniture was adequate, the room clean. To our left stood a nicely carved wooden desk. As we sat, Ruth said, "I came to give you the pictures I took near the grocery store. I also brought a couple of toys for the kids." As she talked, she reached into her bag for the gifts.

Lydia looked at the pictures, pleased. She called the children and Igor, who had gone into the next room. The children came in and thanked Ruth for the gifts. They wanted Jane to join them, but she preferred her mother's lap.

Lydia set the table for tea. She warmed water in a silver-plated samovar that she connected with an extension cord to an outlet on the wall. She brought out various kinds of cookies and rare, delicious jams, made of local berries. She also put on the table a small tin tea can with a label written in Arabic.

As we chatted, Lydia prepared the tea. She opened the small can and removed a few spoonfuls of leaves, placing them inside a nearby teapot. When the water inside the samovar boiled, she poured that into the teapot. The tea scent was sweet, exotic.

"This tea smells great," I said, enjoying the contrast with the earlier soggy odor.

Lydia half-filled our cups with boiling water. Then she added the strong infusion from the pot, which she then covered with an enormous tea cozy. It had the shape of a Russian doll and, standing, hid the teapot entirely with its skirt. The doll was like a *babushka*, an old woman dressed in cheap peasant clothes, with glasses and all, knitting a small blue sweater.

"What brought you to our village?" Lydia asked Ruth after sitting down.

"I love the countryside, the outdoors."

"Don't you prefer Moscow?"

"No, absolutely not," Ruth replied. "I'm an artist. I'm only in Moscow because my husband works there."

"You prefer the countryside to the city? Not me," Lydia said. "But I understand that you need to follow your husband. The same happened to me."

"Really, when?" Ruth asked.

"He works at the army base nearby. He was abroad too, once."

The children popped into the room to dip cookies into a small plate that Lydia had filled with jam. Jane wanted cookies with jam, too.

"Where was Igor?" I felt confident enough to ask. "I was surprised to see that your tea had an Arabic label."

"He brought it from Afghanistan. He worked there as an instructor at a technical institute," Lydia answered.

Igor had been playing with the children but he joined the conversation at this point. I noticed he had combed his hair nicely. "I was in Afghanistan for almost two years. I worked in a military training school, it wasn't really a technical institute."

"His work enabled us to buy a lot of things that we needed for the house and for the children," Lydia added.

"Did you go with your husband?" Ruth asked.

"I only visited, no wives were stationed there. I left the children with my mother and went twice for a month."

Igor opened the top drawer of the nicely carved wooden desk and searched for something. "Look at this." He showed us a picture. In it, he was dressed in a military uniform, surrounded by a few young Afghanis.

"These were my students," Igor pointed to the young-sters surrounding him. "Look how poorly dressed they are." The students looked serious, seemingly fearful of their distinguished company.

"We built this school," Igor continued with pride. "It was a military training center, and the instructor's head-quarters." In the background rose a modern building, three or four-stories high, slightly out of focus.

"Compare the students' clothing with my own," Igor commented, a note of superiority in his voice.

Ruth nodded, listening, but I did not like his remark.

"The Afghanis are so destitute and ignorant," Igor continued. "They live on virtually nothing. We are so much better off in this country."

Ruth nodded again.

"Afghanistan is not a superpower, it's a poor country. What did you expect?" I asked Igor.

"I didn't expect them to live so miserably." Igor turned to me. "But I wanted to go there. It was a great chance to see another country. I realized how much better off we really are here."

Again, I did not like Igor's tone, but I only asked, "Did you enjoy the work, at least?"

"No, not really, I couldn't wait to get back home. But it was a good career move. I only went for the money."

"How noble," I exclaimed. A lot of military personnel did the same around the world, but I was offended by Igor's obvious ethnocentrism. I could see Ruth's face tensing up.

Trying to end the conversation, I asked Igor if I could use the bathroom.

"That's the only bad thing about our house," he said. If he was upset with my comment, he did not show it. "You have to go out to the backyard," he said, and offered to escort me.

"I'm sure you can wait until we get back home," Ruth

said in English, giving me a nasty look.

"Why should I?"

"Laura, please be patient," Ruth pleaded.

"But I want to go now."

"Tea wasn't enough for you, was it? You had to be impolite with Igor, now you want to snoop around." Ruth was aggravated; I followed Igor, ignoring her.

When I returned, Ruth was still upset. "Are you happy now?" she said, again in English. "Have you seen enough? What hidden trophies from Afghanistan have they got?"

I did not reply. We said our good-byes to Lydia and Igor, the children waved from the other room. Igor helped Ruth put Jane in the sled.

"I was afraid to put the family at risk if Sergei followed us. I hadn't counted on your lack of tact," Ruth said as we started to walk back. And she added, "Would you rather have met a dead hero's family, with Igor just a picture on the wall? Or would you have preferred to see his framed photograph on one of the gravestones at the cemetery?"

As we walked through the snow, Ruth led the way pulling along Jane's sled. With the stars as our only company in the dark of the night, Ruth and I did not look at each other, not even once.

Farewell, Dear Friend and Comrade

Keith and I were in Moscow when it was announced that Andropov had died. It was an icy February day with a furious cold wind raging throughout the city. For six months rumors had circulated that General Secretary Andropov was fatally ill and his recent public appearances had, indeed, been cancelled. That glacial morning Keith called me from his American Embassy office to say that news agencies abroad had disclosed Andropov's death.

I turned the radio on. The music was dreary and gloomy all morning long. Oddly, one piece of classical music followed the next, with no announcement of composer, orchestra, or conductor. That was the sign. The music intended to prepare the Soviet population for the news to come—their leader was dead.

The following day, Keith and I joined other diplomats and their spouses to view Andropov's body lying in state in the famous Dom Soyuzov, the House of Unions. The Dom Soyuzov, so designated after the Bolshevik Revolution, had a legendary history. It was a classical stucco building, and a former club of the Russian nobility. Lenin and Stalin's bodies had also lain in state there. Eager to participate in the historical moment, I made sure I was at the embassy in time to go by bus with the first delegation. Doug Stevens, a respected senior officer, headed our group.

"So Andropov is gone," I whispered to Keith softly as

we crossed Pushkin Street approaching the Dom Soyuzov. Hundreds of people surrounded the building, lined up to get in. "I still don't know what he died of."

"Usually the Soviets don't disclose that kind of information," Keith answered.

"Why the big secret?"

"Laura, these issues are considered private matters here."

The bus carrying our delegation was getting closer to the Dom Soyuzov. "How can this be a private matter?" I asked. "Look at the hundreds of people waiting to get in." Considering the arctic freeze that had come upon the city that day, as sharp as the Soviet sickle, the outpouring of public grief was noteworthy.

"By the way," Keith changed the subject, a tone of finality in his voice, "as I mentioned yesterday, a Senate delegation is in town, and we're invited to the reception at the Ambassador's residence. I'd love you to wear that low-cut black dress that you bought in Washington shortly after we got married."

"What does the dress have to do with attending the reception? You know I hate that dress now."

"The embassy is choosing people for a new delegation on arms control and I might want to be a part of it. In any case, I'd love us to be high profile and your dress might help."

"It's a summer dress, décolleté, I'd be frozen to death if I wore it." I already felt goose bumps in my shoulders.

"We can discuss this later," Keith replied as the bus was coming to a halt by the Dom Soyuzov.

The movement around the building was incredible. *Militsioners*, Soviet policemen, stood guard every few feet. *Druzhinniki*, volunteer members of the "People's Patrols," wearing red armbands, kept order. As we got off the bus, a man dressed in black came out of the building and ushered us in. We did not have to wait outside.

Many lines had formed in the entrance hall, and our delegation was assigned the space covered by the wide red carpet. Uniformed guards stood along the winding stairway every six or seven feet. When our line moved a few steps, the guards saluted us. Doug Stevens, a few steps ahead, led our group with impressive dignity.

The line was slowly trudging along, as if we were going to the Gulag Archipelago. The chandeliers decorating the stairway, the adjacent rooms, and the various halls, glittered like jewels hovering in the air. It was mid-morning, but each of them was lit with what seemed a hundred bulbs. And each was covered in delicate black tulle, as if hundreds of widows were crying that day for their beloved leader.

I felt good dressed in a two-piece black suit, the color most people wore. Keith's idea that I should wear the low-cut dress for the reception crept into my mind. But it was one thing to dress in black for a funeral and another to wear a light summer dress that I hated now just to help promote his career.

We finally entered the former ballroom, the so-called Hall of Columns, where the General Secretary's body lay in state. Carnation wreaths were everywhere, the heavy scent making me woozy. At one side, a live orchestra played a dirge that I was unable to identify. As we came closer to the body, a guard positioned some members of our delegation in front of the coffin. In the shuffle, Keith and I ended up next to Doug Stevens in the first row.

And there lay Andropov, less than seven feet away from us—the General Secretary of the Communist Party of the Soviet Union, a most respected former director of the KGB. A man who had died less than fifteen months after taking charge of his country. His face was fully visible. A blanket of white gladioli surrounded his dark suit and shiny shoes.

Keith and I stood still as a sign of respect for the man who had governed the country in which we were living. Behind us, the *narod*, the Russian people, with a blocked view, were told to keep moving. I was grateful for not having fainted from the smell of the flowers. The orchestra played on.

We moved after a few minutes, leaving the room in silence. The exit line was going fast, with Doug Stevens still ahead of us.

As we boarded the bus, I turned to Doug and asked in a friendly voice, "Remarkable scene, wasn't it?"

"Most impressive," Doug replied with a polite smile, he did not seem interested in chatting.

"Aren't you glad I brought you?" Keith touched my arm as we sat down.

"Oh, yes, it was a scene to die for," I said with a glow in my eyes.

"The funeral will take place in two days, then we have the reception."

"Keith, I'll be wearing this two piece suit to the reception. It's perfectly adequate."

"We don't need to discuss this now," Keith answered. His voice had the same note of finality as before. "The day of the funeral is going to be interesting." Keith turned in his seat to get more legroom. "The head of the Funeral Commission is probably going to be the next Secretary General."

"Who is he?"

"An old crow, Konstantin Chernenko."

The day of the funeral was declared a public holiday, and Keith and I sat by the television to watch the ceremony. Only high dignitaries had been invited to Red Square, people like Doug Stevens or higher up. The temperature remained utterly frigid. Moreover, it had snowed during the night and low clouds covered the sky. The air was pale gray as if sympathizing with the historic moment.

The cortege carrying Andropov's body left the Dom Soyuzov heading for Red Square. Like a cannon, the coffin was placed in the middle of a two-wheeled cart, pulled by people on foot. A few relatives marched behind. Government officials, party leaders, various collectives and state organizations, and foreign delegations followed next. Then came the *narod*, trailing after the convoy.

Andropov's daughter wore a silver fox coat and her husband held her by the arm. The widow, we were told, had been spared the long walk. The group's footfalls, as they stabbed the ice on the streets, echoed in the silence.

"What a beautiful fur coat Andropov's daughter has! It seems to have a double function, to sustain her in her grief and warm her at the same time," I exclaimed, eyes glued to the screen.

"Without it she'd freeze in her tracks," Keith said, comfortably sitting in his favorite armchair. And he continued, trying to sound casual, "By the way, Laura, have you tried on the low-cut dress?"

"Keith, please, not again. If you like that dress so much, why don't you wear it yourself?" I tried to sound humorous.

"Don't be silly, you didn't answer my question."

"The dress is too flimsy for this time of the year. Besides," I continued, "every time I wore that dress, men were more interested in my figure than in my words."

"What's wrong with that?"

"Nothing, except that the attention was focused on the wrong place."

"Why do you disappoint me? I brought you to the Dom Soyuzov to see an historical event."

"And I'm supposed to be forever grateful? What am I supposed to do in Moscow, stare at the walls all day long?"

"You could do something for me in return, something I ask you to do."

"I feel used," I said, unable to contain myself.

"No, you don't. I'm only asking you a favor."

I turned to the screen, I needed relief from the conversation. The distance between the Dom Soyuzov and Red Square was under normal circumstances a fifteen-minute walk. But the cortege was taking a long time, its pace slow, meditative.

Keith looked at the screen, too, and then said, "The procession is getting to the podium at Lenin's tomb. All the Politburo members are going to be there. The head of the Funeral Commission will make the first speech."

Andropov was about to be buried by the Kremlin wall. The Politburo members were wearing bulky dark overcoats with woolen scarves tightly tucked in at the neck. Fur hats covered most of their faces. At the center of the podium stood the head of the Funeral Commission, his body heavy and rigid. He had the face of a peasant, with feline eyes.

The cameras moved to the platform where Soviet dignitaries and foreign delegations stood.

"Is Doug Stevens there?" I asked Keith, trying to change the subject.

"I can't see him, but he was probably invited," Keith replied.

Chernenko started to read the eulogy but could hardly speak, he was so frail. He began a phrase, then stopped in the middle and caught his breath. He tried to speak again, read a couple of words, and coughed. The cough was brief, dry. After taking a few breaths, he read on. Spittle came out of his mouth, flying high and long.

He proceeded as best he could, sometimes reading very quickly, trying to finish a phrase, at other times very slowly, buying time to catch his breath. To maintain his equilibrium, he leaned against the podium. One of his hands clasped the written speech tightly; the other searched the balcony for support. At last, he gathered the strength to deliver the last words, "Farewell, dear friend and comrade. May the earth be light on you."

Impressed, I said to Keith, "I have never seen anything like this in my life. Chernenko seems about to die, too. It isn't grief, the man is sick. The Soviet system is beyond my comprehension if they choose this man to be the next Secretary General."

"In a system that's dying, who else but dying men are left to govern?" Keith watched the screen intently from his armchair. And, trying to sound nonchalant, he said, "Laura, do me a favor, go put that dress on. Maybe it doesn't even fit you anymore."

"I'm cold. Watching this ceremony makes me even colder." And I added, "I'll make a deal with you. If you promise that trying on the dress has nothing to do with my wearing it to the reception, I'll do it."

"I promise," Keith said, leaning back in his armchair, at ease now. "That dress always looked great on you."

"Alright, just to please you."

Before changing, I glanced back at the screen. The Politburo members were now saluting the coffin. Chernenko could not lift his hand to his head. He tried to raise it, but it only went half way. He tried a second time and failed a second time. The hand finally met his forehead as he lowered his head. It stayed there for a few seconds, palm facing the dead body.

The cameras turned now to Andropov's widow, who had arrived at the scene. She sobbed by the coffin, opened for a last good-bye. A moment later, she touched her former husband's shoulders, then kissed his forehead and his hands passionately. People stood by her side, gently trying to remove her.

And for as long as she stayed by the corpse, the Politburo members continued the salute. Except for Chernenko. He tried, but he could not hold his hand upright. The cameramen moved away from him every time he brought his hand down.

Finally, a black-suited burial crew maneuvered the ropes to settle the coffin into the grave. The dirge was now the celebrated *Funeral March* by Chopin.

Flattering myself with thoughts that Keith might want to see me in the dress whether I wore it to the reception or not, I went into the bedroom and found it in an old plastic garment bag. As I put it on a shiver ran down my spine. Surprisingly, the dress still fit me. With matching shoes, I returned to the living room, but not without admiring myself in the mirror first.

I could see Keith was excited when he saw me. "Wow, the dress still fits you beautifully. You look terrific."

"Thanks," I said. "I don't even know what crossed my mind when I bought it. Moscow is too cold for it, anyway."

"You look glamorous," Keith said.

"The dress is glamorous," I replied.

"You are glamorous in that dress."

"I'll take it off now. Mission accomplished." I said a few minutes later as I headed for the bedroom.

The ceremonies were almost over when I returned to the living room. The Politburo members looked dejected. Their ages, the freezing temperature, the low gray sky, all seemed to run them down.

"I'm glad this is coming to an end," I told Keith. "I can't stand it any longer."

"The Soviets have a grand sense of tragedy, that's for sure," Keith picked up a book on the Hermitage Museum from the coffee table. Then he added, "Make sure you don't put the dress back in the garment bag."

"Why?"

"Even if you don't wear it, I like to look at it," he said, his eyes piercing my soul.

The following morning Keith told me he was going to work until the reception, which started at 7:30. Could I meet him at his office? From there we would go together to the

Ambassador's residence, Spaso House.

Stupidly, I agonized all day long about what to wear, the low-cut dress or the two-piece suit. One hour I decided in favor of one, the next hour in favor of the other. The dress was not warm enough for the season; besides, I did not like it anymore. But it still fitted me beautifully, giving me an occasion to please Keith.

And more than that, I reasoned, helping promote Keith's career was helping to promote myself as well.

When I entered Keith's office I had my fur coat on, therefore he could not see what I was wearing. When he asked, I did not feel like telling him. I sat in such a way in the car as to make sure that he did not see my outfit. He dropped the subject, he would soon find out.

When we arrived at Spaso House, and as Keith helped me take off my coat in the lobby, I shivered with the cold. Keith immediately greeted Doug Stevens who had just come in.

I said hello to Doug, and the three of us made our way to the spacious living rooms. The place was already crowded and hordes of waiters were serving drinks from large trays. Doug looked at Keith, "Stunning dress your wife has on."

"Thank you," Keith said, looking only at Doug, as if I did not exist.

"It was great to visit the Dom Soyuzov yesterday, such a historical moment," I said to Doug, ignoring his remark about my dress. "Why do you think Chernenko was chosen to succeed Andropov?"

"Maybe the Soviets are training a younger politburo member for the job, and they need someone in between," Doug replied.

"Do you want a drink, Laura?" Keith tried to shift my attention as he helped himself to a glass of wine from a waiter's silver tray.

"I'll have a scotch." Hoping the drink would warm me

up, I sipped it eagerly.

"Someone younger—like who?" I pursued, turning to Doug.

"Someone like Gorbachev. A smart man with new ideas, someone who might want to open the Soviet system. It's still too early to say, Gorbachev needs more seasoning."

"Gorbachev impressed people very favorably when he visited Western Europe recently," I said. "You probably saw Chernenko up close at the funeral. What did you think of him?"

"Laura, you'd better sip your drink, you don't…," Keith shook his head, annoyed that I was keeping Doug's attention.

"Doug, are all men the same?" I asked with a special intonation. I had worn the dress to please Keith, but Keith did not want me in the center stage. I could not even exchange a few words with Doug without Keith growing jealous.

"That I can't say," Doug smiled warmly. Then he added, "Please excuse me. Someone just arrived who I need to talk to." And more intimately, "I'll remember your dress for quite some time."

"See you later, Doug," I smiled.

Turning to Keith I could not contain myself, "You used me. You didn't even want me to talk to Doug. You only wanted him to ogle my body."

"Here's a useful piece of advice," Keith said sternly. "As far as Soviet politics is concerned, behave like a child—be seen and not heard."

Feeling a chill I had anticipated only my dress would bring, I took Keith's remark despondently. Without expecting an answer, I asked firmly, "You think I'm as big a boob as Chernenko, don't you?"

Keith did not reply; instead, he joined the group of people next to us.

At the Kosmos Hotel

Denise and I used to swim regularly at the Kosmos Hotel, but one evening we became fed up with the place. The Kosmos was a tall, cold, glassy building on Prospekt Mira, a few miles from downtown Moscow. Like all enterprises at the time, the hotel was state-owned. Managers, clerks, waiters, and cleaning personnel were all public employees. The Kosmos had a large, attractive swimming pool, usually empty in the late afternoon on weekdays. As we soon discovered, at that time of day the lobby was filled with prostitutes: thin, young, blonde, partly coquettish, partly languid, sometimes both. Inevitably, they wore either American jeans or tight, black mini-skirts.

Some days, getting through the entrance door of the gigantic lobby was a major accomplishment. If so disposed, the porter might let us in after inspecting our diplomatic cards. On other days, however, he would follow us with his eyes as we crossed the lobby to get the hotel's entrance permit at the appropriate bureau. Here, the attendant would ask us if we had hard currency to pay for the swimming ticket because if we did not, we could not swim. With tickets in hand, we would pay at another *guiché*, the *kassa*. If we paid in dollars and the young woman gave us change in Yemenis, as she usually did, a small fight would follow. On a bad day, more than half an hour would be lost just getting through the lobby.

Since we had similar backgrounds, Denise and I became friends the day we arrived in Moscow. She had married an American diplomat, Tony Edmunds, a few months before coming to Moscow.

One day Denise accompanied me to the Kosmos to have a drink at the bar while I swam; dinner at the restaurant upstairs would follow. She wanted to celebrate her first day of work at a Quebec radio station located in Moscow.

We had been to the bar before. It was a crowded place, dark, sleazy, with a cloud of smoke in the air. As people came in, they shared round tables placed indiscriminately close together. At one end of the room, a fairly large window allowed people to watch swimmers in the pool below. As I swam that day, I saw Denise wave a few times, pointing to her watch.

When I met her at the bar later on, the room was fully packed. But from the entrance door I could see that Denise had a special glow in her luminous green eyes. Sitting next to her at the same table was a man, talking. He was older, with greasy hair combed straight to the back. He wore a striped gray suit, pink shirt, and patterned green tie. The fellow was sitting as close to Denise as possible, his shoulders virtually touching hers. Watching from a distance, I smiled wryly.

When I approached them, Denise used the style of introduction reserved for foreigners, "Laura, this is *Gospodin* Ivanov." She used the word *gospodin*, mister, not the word *tovarishch*, comrade. A pack of Marlboros lay near the man's hands and the table's ashtray was filled with cigarette butts. I did not like his looks, his oily hair, let alone the smell of his cologne.

"Nice meeting you," I said nevertheless.

"Can I offer you a drink?" he asked, smiling. His direct gaze revealed a special interest in foreign women, as if he assumed they were all sexually free.

"I'm not sure," I said. "My friend and I planned to have dinner upstairs." I turned to Denise, "What do you think, is there any time for dinner? Why were you pointing at your watch while I was swimming?"

"I was supposed to call Tony earlier, but I kept waiting for you. He might join us for dinner."

Gospodin Ivanov took his chance, "C'mon, sit down, have a drink with us," he said, as he got up to pull an empty chair from a nearby table. When he sat again, he allowed some shoulder distance between himself and my friend.

As I sat down, Denise asked, "Laura, what took you so long at the pool?"

"You wouldn't believe it. My entrance ticket had a time stamped on it, one hour later than the time we arrived, and the *babushka* in charge wouldn't let me in. She was stout, very strong, and insisted that I had to wait. I argued with her that the pool was empty and it didn't make a jot of a difference what time I went in. It took all my powers of persuasion to overcome her dictum, 'Rules are rules, they cannot be bent at your whim,'" I said, imitating the *babushka*'s harsh tone.

"Ah, now I see. Well, was the swim worth it?"

"It was great. Such a large pool, so much space! The worst part, as usual, was the smell. I still don't understand why they put so much chlorine in the water. Maybe they think it acts as a protective measure against AIDS."

"What would you like to drink?" Ivanov asked.

"I'll wait for dinner. I don't want anything now, thanks."

"*Gospodin* Ivanov works for the Ministry of Foreign Trade. He has been to England, Greece, and Cuba. He's a world traveler!" Denise said, addressing me while smiling at Ivanov.

"Yes, indeed, and I love to meet foreigners," he said. "I come here often to meet delegations from abroad. And I get a chance to practice my English."

"What do you do at the Ministry?" I asked.

"I'm on a committee that deals with imports and exports."

"Is that what gives you the opportunity to travel?"

"Yes, indeed. And what do you do? How do you spend your time in Moscow?"

I answered vaguely, "Oh, I stay busy; I swim, I study Russian, I go to parties."

"And your husband, what does he do at the embassy? I imagine he has a good job, no?"

"He works in the political section," I lied.

"Nice job. Importing sugar cane from Cuba is much less glamorous. But I love the travel side of the job, and I loved my studies when I was young."

"Where did you study?"

"At the Academy of Foreign Trade. There were big names there when I was a student. I was born near the Volga in an industrial town. I studied engineering first, then went to work, and after that entered the academy. I studied in the evening."

"Where did you work before?"

"In a food processing plant on the outskirts of Moscow. I became an assistant manager quite young. But it was a boring job with no future." He paused to light another cigarette, then looking first at Denise, he asked, "Tell me, would you two like to go to the movies sometime soon?"

"Who knows, maybe if we meet here again," Denise answered pushing back her golden hair and exposing her pretty ear lobe. I cautioned her, "What about that phone call to Tony? We should get going, shouldn't we?"

She agreed and, turning to Ivanov, said, "It was nice chatting with you." As she got up, she put a few dollars on the table to pay for her drink. *Gospodin* Ivanov addressed her, looking greasy again, "How come you don't even let me pay for your drink?"

Denise smiled and shrugged her shoulders, "In the West, independent women pay for their own drinks."

As we went into the corridor, I asked with a wicked smile, "When I arrived, Ivanov was on your lap. What was going on?"

"You mean he would have liked to be on my lap," Denise said emphatically. She continued, "The space in the bar is tight. We just talked, but I found him sly. There was something about his attitude that I didn't like."

"I agree! What did he tell you when you were alone?"

"I'll tell you later. Let's find a phone first."

We returned to the lobby and asked a heavy female clerk, her dark blue waistcoat bulging from her bust, where could we find a telephone booth.

"Over there," she said, pointing with her index finger, "go straight, turn left, then turn right. Straight on, again, and you'll see it."

We never found the booth. Returning to the lobby, we asked another woman.

"The telephones aren't working. The only phones you can use to call outside the hotel are in the rooms."

"Well, that lady over there could have told us that," Denise replied.

"Am I supposed to guess what my colleague was thinking? She might not have known," the employee answered brusquely, annoyed with the reprimand.

Irked, we headed for the restaurant upstairs. As we entered the large room, I pointed to a telephone on the table by the entrance door. Without hesitation Denise addressed the waiter, "Can I use your phone?"

"Only if you are very, very quick. I cannot let clients use this line."

"It will be only a minute."

"Alright, then," the waiter replied. "This is a favor I'm

doing just for you."

While Denise dialed the number, I looked at my watch. We had wasted twenty minutes worrying about the phone call.

"Tony's finishing some work," she said, hanging up. "If he comes, he'll be here in 45 minutes."

The waiter led us to the furthest possible corner of the room. We had passed more than fifty empty tables, Russians usually dined later. He advised us to choose from the buffet as dinner was not à la carte.

"Here we are in our foreigner's paradise," I said. "The microphones might be just under the table. But who cares, let them know what we think, it might be good for them." I continued, "What do you think, is Ivanov a spy in disguise?"

"He could very well be. Who knows? He likes foreign women, that's for sure."

"Why do you think he does?"

"I can only guess."

"By the way, what did he tell you when you were alone?"

"He said he wanted to practice his English. But he wanted to talk more about me than about him. I was surprised he answered your questions."

"What did he ask you?"

"What I did, Tony's job, what made us want to come to Moscow."

"The guy must be high in the Ministry of Foreign Trade to be here so leisurely at this hour. All that traveling is pretty unusual for a regular Soviet."

"For sure. He's probably a party member, too. Did you see how well dressed he was? Soviet stuff, but good quality."

"Yes, I noticed. Soviets kill for trips abroad, so he must have done something right inside the system to be where he is."

"Probably. I'm hungry, let's get some food at the buffet now."

The food consisted of fish in a watery sauce, meatballs, and mashed potatoes. For dessert there were various bowls of jelly, all the same texture but different colors; some were green, a few orange, and others dark yellow.

A tall, young waiter stood behind the buffet table waiting to serve us. "I'd like a small portion of fish, a small portion of meat, and some mashed potatoes," I said.

"You can have either the fish, or the meat, with the mashed potatoes. But you can have second helpings, if you want to. I'll give you the fish and the potatoes now," he replied.

"No, no. I don't want to get up from the table a second time. I just want a small, a very small portion of each of the three. But I want them now, please."

"I can't. It's either fish or meat and the mashed potatoes."

The waiter proceeded to put fish and mashed potatoes on a plate. I said, "Alright, give me some meat and potatoes, then."

"You could have told me sooner, I already prepared your plate with fish and mashed potatoes."

"I'll take that," Denise intervened, coming to the rescue.

"Aren't there any vegetables?" I asked, trying to sound nonchalant. "We aren't special clients here, but are there any hidden riches in the kitchen?"

"There are no vegetables. This is the middle of winter, what do you expect?" With this answer the waiter virtually threw the plates at us.

We went back to the table. Tony had not arrived, he was probably tied up at work. We started to eat and I asked Denise, "Remember when Ivanov said that he worked in a food processing plant and studied at the Academy for Foreign Trade in the evening? That must have been tough. Besides, just to enroll there must be rather difficult."

"I'm sure, but it opens the way to foreign travel, knowledge of the world outside."

"I imagine he did something important to be able to go to the academy."

"You bet. Maybe his boss at the plant, the head manager, did something wrong or illegal and he reported on him. The same way he might report on us to the KGB now."

"Grim thoughts you have! And what is there to say? I met two women at the Kosmos, one went swimming, the other had a drink with me at the bar. Both husbands work for the American Embassy. What's so interesting about that?"

"Well, he can build on it if we meet again, if we talk again. That's why he invited us to the movies."

"I guess you're right."

"He told me that he's a regular customer here at the Kosmos. The waiter at the bar knew him."

We finished the main course and got up to get coffee. There was none, so we settled for tea. Denise took one of the jelly bowls for us to taste, the orange flavor, and two spoons.

As we sat down again, I saw, to my surprise, that the very *Gospodin* Ivanov we had been discussing was entering the restaurant. He smiled to the waiter at the entrance, someone he obviously knew, stopped to light a Marlboro, and studied the room with ease. His manner was self-assured, confident. He seemed taller than he had at the bar.

Perplexed, I watched him cross the large room in the direction of our table. There was nothing to do. From my vantage point, I barely had time to alert Denise to the approaching visitor. When she replied that he might only want to have dinner, as we did, I warned her that he was walking straight to our table.

He approached us smiling, "May I join you?" Without waiting for an answer, he sat down.

"We're leaving soon," I replied.

"Why? What's the rush? By the way, how was dinner? I love their meat stuffed in cabbage leaves."

"Dinner was okay, nothing to brag about," Denise answered.

"Well, would you two care for some cognac?" Again without waiting for a reply, he waved to the waiter. From a distance, the waiter made the shape of a bottle with his hands, to which *Gospodin* Ivanov nodded.

Looking at me, he proceeded, "You know, I haven't told you yet, but my Spanish is as good as my English. I loved visiting Cuba, I wanted to learn the language. Young women there hang around outside the discos waiting for a foreigner to bring them in and pay for a drink. They dance like no one else in the world."

Suddenly, he started singing the famous song by Eduardo Saborit, "*Cuba, qué linda es Cuba.*" His voice was good, warm. His Spanish was near fluent. I smiled, surprised. *Gospodin* Ivanov added, looking at the two of us, "You know, Cuban women are heavenly, really beautiful."

"From what you say, they must be great at making love!" Denise exclaimed.

"Oh, yes, they are, they certainly are. They're fantastic, totally uninhibited. I had the time of my life. "*Guantanamera, guajira, Guantanamera...,*" he started again, singing another well-known melody in Spanish. The warmth of his voice was quite alluring.

He poured some cognac into the glasses the waiter had brought with the bottle and started to sip slowly, enjoying the flavor, deliberately making smacking sounds with his lips. He turned to me, "Drink some cognac, it's from Armenia. You'll enjoy it."

When I told him I did not drink cognac, he continued as if he had not heard, "I'm going to try this jelly, if you don't mind. I really like it. I'm delighted that the two of you started it but didn't finish." He picked up one spoon and tried the jelly, then he picked up the other and tried another mouthful, licking the spoon slowly.

"We didn't like it," Denise said.

"Really? So much the better for me. It gives me the opportunity to taste it. Plus, I relish the two spoons that you ate from. It's been a lucky day," he added, savoring the dessert.

Denise winked at me. Ivanov noticed and winked back. I burst out laughing, unable to restrain myself.

Ivanov looked around the dining room now, pleased with himself. People were slowly filling the other tables. He soon said with a smile, "Excuse me but I have to leave you for a few minutes," and got up and left.

As soon as he disappeared, I said to Denise, "Let's go, this adventure has already gone one step too far for my liking. Ivanov is up to something. If Tony is on his way, we can wait for him in the car. This is the perfect chance, Ivanov must have gone to the bathroom."

We called the waiter and asked for the bill. He used an abacus to add the total, moving the balls quickly from right to left.

We were about to get up when Denise turned to me, uneasy. "Look, Laura, look at the napkin in Ivanov's place."

"What?"

"Look at it." I looked closely, and there, in between its white folds, was a hotel key with a tag attached, indicating a room, 963.

"The bastard, what nerve!" I said. "And he likes foreigners, hmm, and he speaks Spanish, hmm? Come on, Denise, let's go." As we got up, the waiter approached us with the bill. Denise was treating me. The waiter started arguing about the tip. "This is all you're leaving after I let you use the phone?" While they hashed it out, I had an impulse. I grabbed the key and stuck it in my pocket.

Gospodin Ivanov was nowhere to be seen.

On our way out, with the usual prostitutes hanging around the lobby, I told Denise I had the key to room 963 in my pocket. "What shall I do?" I asked her. "Find a garbage can? Or give it to one of these women? I can say that a friend of mine will be happy to pay three times her price tonight. She only needs to bring a friend to watch."

"Suit yourself," Denise said with another wink in her green eyes as we hurried out of the Kosmos.

Crescendo

From my kitchen window, I could not see the *militsioner* by the building's entrance gate. But I knew the Soviet policeman was always there, day and night, night and day. Every time I left or entered the diplomatic compound, he stood there, watching. Sometimes he strolled around his booth to warm up with a bit of exercise. At other times, he stayed inside looking through the tiny square window on top.

Usually my moods dictated how I treated him. If in a reasonable disposition, I greeted him. If feeling low, I passed by without looking in his direction. But his presence could not be ignored. In the long winter months he wore a huge, well-fitted, gray overcoat. The earflaps of his *shapka*, the gray fur hat, covered his ears and hung down to his chin. The communist insignia, a juxtaposed hammer and sickle, stood out boldly on the hat's front. Solid black, knee-high leather boots and voluminous black gloves completed his outfit.

He always stood inside the wire fence that enclosed the building where foreigners like Keith and I lived. He worked in daily shifts and, after several hours of surveillance, a clone replaced him. The same routine ensued, it did not make any difference who was there. These were big brothers of sorts—looming, overshadowing, threatening.

One crisp Monday morning in early December, the sort of clarity in the air that only follows a recent blizzard, I saw from one of my windows the first wave of a huge number of trucks. Over the following days more and more trucks arrived. By Thursday, a tremendous number of vehicles, in myriad shapes and forms, had parked around the building. Before my eyes gathered, unexpectedly, cattle trucks, dump trucks, pick-up trucks, tractors, and wagons. All of them worn out, dirty, decrepit. Against the characteristic quiet of the Bolshaya Ordynka neighborhood, the scene was definitely unusual.

The trucks arrived and parked on both sides of the street, on two sides of the building. To fit in, they needed to squeeze by each other through the recent slush. I could hear the sound of wheels whirling and spinning against the muddy pavement. Sometimes a vehicle moved only to be instantly replaced by another; a heavy horn blared. Sometimes the trucks double-parked, and the drivers talked loudly as they maneuvered. Unfortunately, the trucks stayed day after day, like *militsioners*, fully blocking the space around the street beyond the wire fence.

By the end of the week the building seemed besieged. Through my windows, I could only see vehicles, mud, drivers running back and forth, fumes escaping exhaust pipes, and chaos. I was living inside a junkyard.

I asked a few neighbors if they knew what was happening. I visited my friend Rose, who also lived in the building and had adopted a baby girl a few months before, but she had no idea what was going on. I questioned Keith at work. I even called the administrative section of the American Embassy, but no one had an explanation for the sudden influx of trucks.

Soon I realized that the drivers kept the engines on all day. And I also noticed that they were sleeping inside the vehicles at night—engines still running. I felt no pity that they might need to keep warm against the freezing temperatures or assure themselves that the motors would start again when needed. For me, the level of noise was intolerable. It was a constant drone that would not go away.

One night unable to fall asleep, I expressed my anguish to Keith. Cool as ever, he told me to put some pillows over my ears. I did, but it did not help. One hour later he advised me to take a sleeping pill. I tried that as well, but to no effect. Keith warned me that he thought I was overreacting, that I should calm down, but his remark only intensified my distress.

It was not only the noise and the general atmosphere that I could not stand. It was as if the exhaust pipes' fumes had seeped inside the apartment, into my own bedroom. Petrol, metal, and chemicals were all mixed up to form a revolting odor. I felt that my body, even my soul, was slowly being contaminated by a deadly substance, and its name was carbon monoxide. I sensed that I was being poisoned, but when I tried to vomit nothing came out. Anger started to build inside of me, larger than life, scary.

The following morning, I decided to confront the *militsioner* standing at the building's entrance gate. I felt feisty, ready for an argument. Approaching the policeman, I returned his salute with a contemptuous smile.

"Can you explain what's going on? What are all these vehicles doing here?" I lashed out.

"I don't know," he answered indifferently, keeping his usual composure. "For traffic questions you had better contact the nearest GAI."

"You have a telephone in your booth, why don't you call the traffic police yourself? After all, it's easier for you."

"I can't."

"Why not?" I persisted.

"I can only use the telephone for my work."

"And using the phone for this reason is not part of your work? I don't understand what is going on, I asked you a question. You people are always around. Surely you know, or can find out, what's going on."

"If you want an explanation, you'd better call or go to GAI yourself."

I turned around and headed home, furious. Inside, I picked up the phone and called Rose, "Do you want to have some fun?" I asked. "I just talked to the *militsioner* downstairs, and he told me I needed to go to the local GAI if I wanted to find out what's going on outside. Do you want to come along? I know where the place is."

"Alright, give me half an hour and I'll be ready. I need to bring Rosalie, I don't have a baby-sitter today."

"That's fine, let's see how GAI reacts to two foreign women and a baby girl. Rosalie might come in handy, Russians love children."

As I drove slowly by the *militsioner*'s booth to exit the gate, the three of us inside the car, the phone inside the booth rang piercingly. It was the most caustic pitch conceivable. I looked at Rose, a dark smirk on my face, "Here is the *militsioner*'s opportunity to report exactly where we are going. Today, he doesn't even need to call someone already parked in the area to follow us."

"You won't believe this, Laura," Rose said, "after we adopted Rosalie, every time I passed the booth with her in the car, the telephone rang. It only rang when I passed with her, not when I passed alone. It was so weird!"

"The people watching from the building in front probably called the booth. This is a society of full employment, after all, they need to keep people busy."

"It's the only possible explanation. Otherwise, how could the timing be so perfect?"

I drove out carefully. The mud had transformed the ground into a gigantic layer of dirty sand. It was extremely slippery; cars zigzagged everywhere. Dirty ponds of melted snow looked like wells into which we might fall. Crossing Oktyabrskaya Square I looked at Lenin's gigantic statue, his index finger commanding Soviets to building socialism. As we passed, a *militsioner* stood in the middle of the road, exactly between the two lanes of traffic, watching.

"These guys are like ants, everywhere," I muttered, shaking my head.

Like others, this *militsioner* carried a black, heavy stick in his right hand. He moved the stick back and forth in a circular motion as the traffic crawled by. Sometimes the stick formed only a half circle, sometimes a full one. The stick moved fast, so the policeman needed a great amount of dexterity to stop its movement half way. But thus entertained, he seemed to have all the time in the world.

The GAI branch was on a small side street fairly close to the square. A sign on top of the building indicated the location by a dismal bunch of misaligned letters. We parked at the main entrance, there was a space in front of the building. As we entered, the door squeaked loudly.

The place was virtually empty. We found two deputies inside a small guiché, attended by two secretaries. The two women were eagerly discussing a colleague's recent surgery to remove her uterus. If the office had been warned of our arrival, they did not seem to mind. I addressed one of the policemen, stating that we wished to talk to the *nachalnik*, the head of the station. Realizing that we were foreigners, he told us that we would be announced immediately.

While waiting, I decided to poke around. A small corridor to the left led to a door with the inscription "Lenin's Room," which I entered. On each side stood two huge placards. One listed the directives of the latest Party Congress. The head sign stated: "The directives of our Party Congress—we fulfill!" The second one was dedicated to Dzerzhinsky, the founder of the CHEKA, the first Soviet security apparatus, later renamed NKVD, and finally called KGB after Stalin's death. I gazed at the series of pictures all bearing a title: "Dzerzhinsky as a child playing with his parents,"

"Dzerzhinsky in primary school," "Dzerzhinsky at his marriage ceremony," and "Dzerzhinsky receiving various foreign dignitaries." It was as if the fellow was still alive.

Soon the policeman returned to tell us to follow him upstairs. We were obviously heading to the supervisor's office. On the second floor stood several wood benches placed along the walls, presumably for people to sit on while waiting. The corridor had a narrow green and red carpet that led directly into the *nachalnik's* office. The policeman knocked deferentially at one door and, as he opened it, I realized that the carpet ended only under the boss's desk.

We came into a large room and faced a jolly, fat fellow sitting at his desk. He greeted us with a smile on his round red face. As the deputy pulled three chairs in front of his desk, the boss addressed Rose, "Please, please, sit down. Yes, put the baby in your lap." He turned to his deputy impatiently, "The baby doesn't need an extra chair!"

And, pleasantly, addressing us both, "I hear that you live in Bolshaya Ordynka Street and have a traffic problem. What can I do for you?"

I addressed him with the traditional Russian polite phrase, "Senior Lieutenant, we came here to disturb you because..." and began to explain the chaotic traffic situation around the building where we lived.

"Oh, someone should have told you what is going on. I don't understand why you don't know yet—but you are foreigners, that's why. With what embassy, may I ask?"

We answered him.

"With the American Embassy? Really? I never had such distinguished company in this office! Well, let me tell you what is going on. There is a truck repair factory near your building on a small side street. In order to fulfill the yearly plan, and since the factory is obliged to repair a certain number of vehicles per year, it usually gets very busy during December, the last calendar month. Drivers bring trucks

from all over Russia, get a repairs voucher, and have to wait
around for their turn. If spare parts are needed, it might
take them a few days, sometimes even weeks. It's the same
scene every year."

"I would never, never, have thought of that," I answered.

"You can rest assured that by the end of the month, the
latest by mid-January, everyone will be gone. Believe me,
it's the same chaos every year, but it also ends every year."

"We have to wait from three to six weeks? I might as
well move to the moon. I need you to do something about
this, now!" I insisted.

"Tell me, are there already a lot of trucks?"

"Yes, there are. Why don't you come with us and see for
yourself?"

"Good idea. I'm short of time, but I'll accompany you ladies with great pleasure. I've always craved the company of
foreigners. And I have so very few chances to meet them,"
he said with a broad smile.

Rose and I exchanged an amused glance as we went
down the decaying stairway. Maybe we were finally getting somewhere. Downstairs, the *nachalnik* told us that his
driver would follow our car. Back in Bolshaya Ordynka, he
instructed the driver to remain in the car as we talked in the
street.

"Yes, indeed, the movement seems a bit out of control,"
he acknowledged.

"At night it's awful," I added, since I had found a sympathetic ear.

"By the way, do you ladies smoke?" the supervisor
asked. "I love Marlboros, it's a favorite brand of mine, very
difficult to find here."

"I've got a package at home. Wait a minute, I will go inside to get it for you," I said, leaving Rose and Rosalie alone
with the fellow. As I walked away, I heard him ask Rosalie's

patron saint's name.

Making my way through the thick, dirty slush, struggling to keep my balance, I soon returned with the package wrapped inside a plastic bag. I kept it in my hand.

"Well, I have to go now," the lieutenant announced. "And don't worry, ladies. I will make sure this problem gets under control."

As we shook hands and he opened the door of his car, I slipped the package into his seat. I added, smiling, "Don't forget, it gets worse during the night, alright?"

"I'll take care of it personally. By the way, here is a telephone number if you need to call us. We have teams on duty twenty-four hours a day." He handed me a handwritten number on a piece of paper.

For a few days the traffic around the building was, indeed, under control. Rose and I discussed happily how the *nachalnik* was no phony, after all. But, as the days passed, our victory slowly faded.

One night, well past midnight, I found myself unable to sleep again. I picked up the telephone number I had been given. I called once, I called twice. I called again twenty minutes later. No one answered. Keith had returned from an exhausting trip and was fast sleep. When I woke him up, he told me, annoyed, that there was nothing he could do about the noise outside.

I moved to the living room and drank some wine while listening to Vivaldi's Four Seasons. But it did not work. The weird feeling was returning. I could hear Keith snoring once in a while, and even that sound was upsetting. I dreaded the solitude, the hours awake, the long night. Looking out of one window I had a strange impression. Below the stars, under the dim streetlights, there was only desolation, slush, smoke, and the monotonous truck motors at work; worst of all was that pestilent smell.

I looked at the clock. Half an hour had already passed.

Suddenly, I felt deranged, out of my mind. And a compelling force dictated that I challenge the *militsioner* again. Maybe he will think I will go insane if he does not act, I thought to myself. Raving, I started to dress. To face the hard cold outside, I needed to use several layers of clothing, my boots and gloves, and the fur hat.

I tore down the stairs and thrust out the front door. Charging recklessly ahead, I almost fell in the courtyard's mud. The *militsioner* happened to be inside his booth, so I made a daring gesture. I threw his door wide open without knocking.

The man was awake, sitting on a tiny bench on the right side, with a blanket covering his legs. Opposite him, lying on a small shelf on the other side, stood the telephone and a small thermos. Several empty coffee cups lay around. Astonished, he told me forcefully to back off. And removing his blanket in haste, he swaggered out immediately.

"I already discussed this situation with your colleague," I shouted. "GAI doesn't answer my calls. My husband doesn't seem to care. Can't you do something about this noise? I truly cannot sleep."

"No, there's nothing I can do. You must contact GAI again tomorrow."

"But what about now? Why don't you call them?"

"I cannot use the phone for that purpose. You have to call yourself."

"Alright!" I replied beyond control, "I'm going to stand here with you until you make that damned phone call."

Unperturbed, the *militsioner* looked out at me in the dark. In slow gear as if in an old movie, I saw him trying to find a package of cigarettes in his pockets. When he found it, he stroked it over and over again, as if fondling something, someone. Then, he inspected the cigarette tips carefully, finally deciding on one; he took it out, and pushing it back and forth against the package, straightened it to the perfect upward position. Then he reached into his pocket for matches. With the tiny box in his hands he tried to light one, but the wind blew it out. He tried a second time and failed again. He could have turned the other way round, but I suspected that he did not want to have me at his back. So he curved his left hand like a shell, and placing the small box at its center, tried to light another match. Again he failed. After half a dozen tries, he finally succeeded.

Next, he took deep, long puffs; as he smoked, he scrutinized me earnestly. I looked straight at him, eyes on fire. He puffed back. His expression was somber, but his eyes now had an amused look. He did not send the smoke directly into my face, but almost. I could practically smell his breath.

It was just a week before the winter solstice. Time itself seemed to have stopped as light snow started to fall. With my gloves I brushed aside a few flakes that had fallen into my eyes. I, too, wanted to see him clearly. And examining his expression, I realized that he would let me stand there until my pupils iced over.

I looked at the hammer and sickle on his *shapka*, and images of the Second World War crossed my mind. I saw Soviet soldiers eating their own shoe soles, persevering against every possible hardship. I realized their stamina against the cold weather and their endurance in the face of adversity. With the wind blowing that night, I would freeze—not him. With his patience, I might go crazy—he would be fine. His expression might drive me to suicide—but he would stand still, lucid.

I decided to turn around and run home again. Inside, there was nothing I could possibly do. I paced the living room for a while, back and forth like a prisoner, a lion in its cage. Had I slapped the *militsioner*, as I almost did, I would have felt much, much better. Hysterical, I came to believe that hell, the blaze of hell itself, might be a better place than where I was. The monotonous, high-pitched sound of the engines running outside contrasted too sharply now with Keith's heavy sleep, the silence in the bedroom. Suddenly, I turned Vivaldi to a deafening pitch. Then, I ran to the tub in the bathroom, filled our largest pan with icy water and, reaching the bed, threw it lavishly, deliriously, on Keith's face, head, and neck.

When Alliluyeva Returned

I came home a bit earlier than usual that afternoon, I wanted to hear Oksana, our maid, humming her favorite songs. Oksana not only had the sweetest of voices, but also the endearing habit of humming as she went along in her work, tune after tune, gently, no words. Oksana was a mother-earth personality of Ukrainian peasant stock, with large bones and hair tied up in a bun, already in her fifties. The woman had a palpable affection for me: she talked about my delicate hands, something no one had ever noticed; and, greatest of gifts, she was able to find in Moscow anything I might need. Moreover, Oksana always addressed me as *madame*—she pronounced the word with a French accent—and that made me feel like the Queen of Sheba.

Oksana was busy setting the table for a luncheon I was hosting the following day. I had pleased her a few weeks earlier by finally going to Passage in Petrovka Street to buy a white tablecloth with matching napkins. Oksana had wanted a plain, white tablecloth for a long time: "*Tolko byeluyu madame, tolko byeluyu,*" she had suggested many times, "Only white, *madame*, only white." She despised my habit of using colorful tablecloths and covering resistant stains with bread baskets and hot plates. Oksana insisted that stains on white cloth could always be removed with the powerful local bleach.

Oksana was impeccable at her job. The Soviet government had trained her at a professional school; like all maids, she was given to us by UPDK, the Soviet Foreign Ministry office in charge of all services for the diplomatic corps. My long-lasting method of setting tables lacked, obviously, the distinguished style she envisioned for her mistress.

These were Oksana's happiest moments at our house, the eve before a luncheon or a dinner party. In more than one way, a party at our house was a party, mainly, for Oksana. The harder the work, the more delighted she was. Oksana was in the living room—queen in her beehive—polishing the table's dark wood as if preparing for a military operation. The white tablecloth required, for her, an impeccably clean table, one that shone like a mirror. By the sideboard she had already placed an array of dishes, plus all the silverware and glasses I owned. Such a large display was unnecessary—six people had been invited for lunch—but, without doubt, Oksana enjoyed touching my finest possessions. There were glasses for water, red and white wine, even champagne, the last ones certainly unnecessary for this event. Oksana also had arranged in another cupboard the white napkins to be placed on the plates. She had elaborately folded them vertically, pointing up, as if they were doves, doves whose wings reached for the sky.

When Oksana heard my compliments on the beautiful napkins, she lowered her eyes and explained in her coy manner that only in white would the doves look so graceful. A statement that I could only corroborate. After all her preparations, how could I possibly explain that the luncheon the following day did not require such effort? I wanted Oksana to know that her work was appreciated.

Oksana's demeanor was something I had never experienced with anybody else, anywhere. First, she had peculiar, dark-green eyes, a green that sometimes turned gray; I had never seen eyes of that color before. But it was the color of her eyes combined with the movement of her eyelids that made her face so special. If she wanted to talk, she would keep her eyelids open; if she wanted to change the course of a conversation or even end a subject, she would either semi-close or fully close them. Her eyelids functioned like the shutters of village houses in Portugal: communication with the outside world depended on the dweller's decision to open or close them.

As Oksana and I chatted away, the phone rang. I hoped the call would end quickly for I wanted to enjoy Oksana's company. As I left the living room, Oksana started to hum gently the familiar folk song "*Ochi chornye*," "Dark Eyes." Picking up the receiver, I recalled the words: "Dark eyes, passionate eyes, fiery eyes ...!"

Vera, a dear Russian friend, was on the other end of the line, her voice as tense as always. Immediately I was transported to another world. Vera and her family were *otkazniki*, people who were refused an exit visa each time they applied to leave the Soviet Union; the Americans called them refuseniks. Vera and her husband Dmitri were frequently invited to embassy receptions, therefore I knew they were "good." In Moscow, a "good contact" meant something unequivocal. These people accepted embassy invitations because they were starved for open discussion of current events; in most cases they were not spies. Members of the intelligentsia, Vera and her husband had lost their jobs after applying for visas to leave the country.

I enjoyed Vera's music, her messy apartment, her two young boys. Vera and I visited each other often, she wanted everybody to know that she did not fear associating with a member of the American Embassy community.

"Hi Laura. How are you?" Vera said in her usual hurried voice as soon as I picked up the phone. She did not wait for my reply, "Listen to the big news. Stalin's daughter, Svetlana Alliluyeva, was allowed to return to our country. A friend of a journalist called, she's already given a couple of press conferences in Moscow."

Vera might be a refusenik—fallen from grace with the Soviet government—but she kept her former high contacts.

"Are you sure?" I asked uneasily.

"Of course I'm sure. One doesn't joke about such matters in this country. The government just reinstated her Soviet citizenship. Turn on your TV, *Vremya* will probably announce the news later on."

"I'll check it, don't worry, you know how much I love that program!" And I exclaimed, "This is incredible."

"She's brought Olga, her daughter from an American father, someone called Peters. The girl's about thirteen. The Soviets have given her Soviet citizenship; the girl doesn't even speak a word of Russian."

"Olga has an American father and the Soviets gave her citizenship?"

"It seems they did." Vera sighed. "Can you imagine how I feel? Svetlana Alliluyeva, Stalin's daughter—the man responsible for sending about twenty million people to their grave—is allowed back in this country. The woman was a defector, the vilest of crimes for the Soviets. But we, who have done nothing wrong, aren't allowed to leave this place."

"Depressing news," I paused. "It must be difficult to be locked up in a jail that happens to be your own country."

"But this isn't all. I have more news. Sit down before I tell you," Vera continued.

"What?"

"Did you sit down yet?"

I put aside Dostoevsky's *Demons* lying on the chair. "Yes, I did. Tell me."

"She's going to be your neighbor, she's moving to Bolshaya Polyanka Street."

"That's not possible!"

"I'm telling you. Make sure you watch *Vremya* this evening. I have to go now, the boys are hungry. I'll talk to you later."

After we hung up, I ran to the living room and turned on the television. Oksana looked at me, sensing my mood change; I told her that a friend had mentioned important news. Oksana lowered her eyelids, closing the shutters. She did not ask what the news was, or who had called.

Because I had gotten Oksana through UPDK, part of her job was to report my activities to the Soviet government, who visited me, who called, what I had in the apartment, and so on. But Oksana never asked any questions, I had the impression she preferred not to know. Oksana's eyelids spoke more than her silences. The appropriate attitude, she had figured out, was to close the shutters.

I moved to the next room, picked up *Demons* and read for a while with the television volume low. The Soviet propaganda film on peasant collectivization did not interest me.

When Keith arrived home a couple of hours later, we discussed the events of the day while he changed in the bedroom. Someone had called the embassy with the news, Keith was informed. A bit later, Oksana helped me place the dinner on a small table in the living room and returned to the kitchen; it crossed my mind that she had left the kitchen door open on purpose. Soon *Vremya* would be on, Keith and I were glued to the television screen.

The program seemed even slower than usual. We thought Alliluyeva's return might be the first news item but it was not, we were wrong. We watched impatiently, expecting after each item that the next one would break the story; after all, the woman had given press conferences upon her return. But there was no news of Stalin's daughter.

Just as Keith and I were speculating that, after all, Svetlana's return was not going to be revealed to the public, the announcement came on close to the end of the program, just before the sports news.

The anchorman read his statement with the usual wooden voice and posture. He referred to Stalin's daughter merely as Svetlana Alliluyeva, her father was not mentioned. No picture was shown. The report said only that Svetlana Alliluyeva—she had used for many years her mother's maiden name—had returned to Moscow after many years abroad. And that she had returned at her own request.

At a press conference for a handful of journalists, the report went on, Svetlana Alliluyeva stated that she had not had a single moment of freedom in the West. The West had only been interested in commercializing her books and her persona. She had returned to Moscow because of her disillusionment with the West. She added that in Russia, her motherland, her daughter Olga would have the best chance for a good upbringing.

That was all. A few minutes after the announcement ended, the phone rang. It was Vera again.

"You see how well informed I am? Svetlana was a public embarrassment in Moscow. But now she's giving the government good propaganda. An opportunity to show that life abroad is not as fulfilling as some people here might think—or wish."

"The Soviets even take advantage of the words of a traitor!"

"I hear that the poor woman is practically insane," Vera added.

"I wonder what Svetlana means when she said that she had no freedom in the West," I asked.

"What she means is that she didn't have a free moment from the shopping mall! She made a fortune with her books, lived in mansions, had servants," Vera was sarcastic.

"Why're the Soviets allowing her back in?"

"She's Stalin's daughter and she wants to return here. This means a lot for the Soviet government. The government is praising Stalin as a strategic genius now."

"I see."

"The misinformation in this country is appalling," Vera continued, bleak. She mimicked the TV announcer's voice, "Svetlana thinks this country is better than the West; Svetlana thinks her daughter will have the best education here; Svetlana wanted to return on her own free will."

The long wait for emigration was taking a heavy toll on Vera. But the rest of the family had been affected as well. Dmitri had lost his university job; in order to make a living, he was ghostwriting academic articles for a former colleague. The family was rotting: financially, emotionally, and physically.

"Vera, I feel badly for you. The closed borders of this country apply only to some families."

"You see?"

"As difficult as it might be, try to cope with your chains. You are locked up here, but you still have a little room to maneuver."

Vera started to cry softly.

"I have people for lunch tomorrow and Oksana, my maid, is still here. But instead of the *madame* she pictures me as, I feel as curious as a French concierge."

"Why?" Vera stopped crying, my remark interested her.

"Haven't you heard how French concierges are always interested in everyone else's life?" I asked. "Well, since your first call, I've developed a huge fantasy."

"About what?"

"This is going to sound utterly stupid. But I've been imagining that I'm going to meet Svetlana in the street one of these days."

"Not likely!"

"How do you know? It could happen. I'm sure she wants to stroll in the old neighborhood, walk around. Even buy bread in the nice shop at the corner of Bolshaya Polyanka, the only one around here that has fresh bread every day. I'm sure a Politburo member lives in the vicinity."

"Who knows what the woman wants?! Svetlana lived with her father in the Kremlin, your neighborhood is the neighborhood of her youth. Stalin was very fond of her, he even called her his little sparrow. At that time, his poor wife had already committed suicide."

"I'm going to spot the woman one day, you can be sure of that. I've seen pictures of her: she is in her mid-fifties, plump, and has a vulgar face. Her eyes are like small almonds, they seem almost Asian."

"Good description."

"I'm sure her foreign clothes will give her away. Do you know what her daughter looks like? Could you get a recent picture of them?"

"They lived in England for several years, maybe you could find a picture in the British newspapers."

"Great idea."

"What's your interest in Alliluyeva, anyway? It seems so morbid!"

"I'm seeing history in the making. It's not every day that I might spot Stalin's daughter around the corner, the real thing, flesh and blood. In my own neighborhood. It's haunting."

"I grant you, it is." Vera continued, "I've got to go. But before I hang up: what did Oksana say when she heard the news?"

"I haven't gone to the kitchen yet. "

"Ask her, will you? I'm interested."

"Alright."

"Good-bye. When I stop by next week, I'll show you where Svetlana lives."

I made my way to the kitchen and pretended to see what Oksana was doing. She did not need supervision, I only wanted to find out if she had heard the news.

Oksana was very flushed. She was finishing an elaborate dish of crabmeat with mayonnaise and sour cream which could have explained the sweat on her forehead. I praised her work and then remarked on her red face. Oksana did not look at me directly, and her eyelids were half-closed. I took this as a sign that she had overheard the news.

"Mmm, big news in your country today, Oksana. Stalin's daughter has returned to Moscow. The little sparrow is back in the nest." Deliberately I kept silent, and then continued, "What do you make of that?"

"Da, *madame*, da," Oksana replied unhurriedly as she nodded with her head, "yes, *madame*, yes." She kept her eyelids low, the shutters might close entirely, I was not sure yet. I might be out of luck, she might not say anything else.

"Oksana, be frank. What do you think brought Stalin's daughter back to this country?"

"*Rodina eto rodina*," Oksana said as she opened her shutters. "The motherland is the motherland." And she proceeded, "We all know there is nothing like it."

"Is that a good enough reason for the tyrant's daughter to return?"

"It's the best of reasons! Svetlana Alliluyeva discovered her love for the motherland; she wanted to return, the government let her in. What more is there to discuss?"

"The little sparrow was a defector, she didn't just take a trip abroad. You know that in the West she published books against this country—don't you?"

"But she repented. We all deserve a second chance; and she has gotten hers. I know she suffered very much in the West."

"Suffered? How?"

"She missed the motherland, the worst of punishments."

"What about all the money she made abroad?"

"Nothing could make up for the emptiness in her heart. Nothing. Believe me, *madame*, this is why she came back: she was homesick."

Oksana had given me the official view, the little sparrow had many voices now. Before she left, she asked me if she could wear lace gloves and a starched maid's cap to serve lunch the following day. She had also bought new, red, high-heeled shoes, much more appropriate footwear, she informed me, than the white canvas boots worn by maids. The red shoes would better match the dark blue uniform. She would show me the items beforehand, she wanted my approval of her outfit.

A few weeks later Vera called again, her voice distressed as usual. This time she wanted to go for a walk, a sign that she had something confidential to share. We went for a stroll in my neighborhood.

"So, have you seen Svetlana yet?" she asked, a bitter tone to her voice.

"No, I haven't. But I must confess, I'm still hoping. Will you show me where she lives?"

We left Bolshaya Ordynka, heading west to Bolshaya Polyanka Street.

"This is the building," Vera indicated with her eyes. My Soviet friends did not point with their fingers, they feared the consequences if someone in an official capacity happened to be watching. "She is above the publishing house *Molodaya Gvardia*."

"Unbelievable. I never thought we would have such distinguished company!" I said with sarcasm.

"Your 'distinguished' is debatable," Vera answered.

"You know what I mean, Vera." And I continued, "Alliluyeva's books are an insult to the Soviet system. Why would she return, freely, to her jail?"

"Only God knows. The public view is that she was homesick, that she couldn't stand to live away any longer.

"That's exactly what Oksana said."

"You see!? And there might be another reason. In 1967 she left behind her two older children from two previous marriages. Maybe she wants to see them before she dies."

"Her return here seems like going back to a bad marriage. Only someone insane would do it."

"People say that she has been very depressed recently."

"Do you think she'll be able to travel freely? Come and go as she wants?"

"Of course she will. There're only a handful of us who're stuck here," Vera had a grim tone to her voice.

"How sad!"

"The damage that Stalin did to this country is irreparable. Once my mother told me that my grandmother made the best paskha at Easter. But the recipe was lost forever, one day my grandmother destroyed it. Even evidence of how to make a cake to celebrate a religious holiday, if forgotten in some old drawer, was enough for a knock on the door in the middle of the night."

"Jesus Christ!"

"Laura, it wasn't to discuss Svetlana or her wicked father that I wanted to see you," Vera said after a pause, her eyes turning murky.

"That much I guessed. To discuss Svetlana we could have stayed inside."

"Dmitri and I are tired of waiting for our exit visas, and we've decided to demonstrate in front of the Gogol statue, next to the Ministry of the Interior. We're bringing the children with us."

"That seems dangerous." Suddenly I could hear Misha, Vera's oldest son, playing the piano; I had never heard a child play with such sorrow.

"We know—but how long can we go on waiting? The biggest danger is for the boys. We can lose custody of them if the government decides to bring us to court. The judge might want to prove that we engaged them in anti-Soviet propaganda."

"That would be horrible. You must feel totally hopeless if you are ready to take such a step. Risking the loss of your children!" I turned to Vera and held her in my arms, tears were rolling down her face.

"We are at a loss," she answered, determined. "If things go wrong we need independent witnesses who saw exactly what happened. Will you come to our demonstration?"

"Count on me, I'll be there. Fortunately your government can't hurt us, they can only expel Keith and me—a blessing in disguise, I suppose. I'll be there, I'm safe with my diplomatic passport."

"Our friend Grisha will let you know the exact day and time. I have to rush back home now."

We said good-bye and Vera entered the Oktyabrskaya metro station. She had gotten thinner, her back arched more than before. Once in a while extraordinary things appeared for sale near the metro entrance. This time an older man had a huge, nineteenth-century scale. People had lined up and were paying a few kopecks to be weighed.

Weeks passed and early one morning I got word of the day and time of Vera's demonstration.

A friend drove the family and dropped the four of them in Gogol's Square, speeding away soon afterwards. The family walked towards the statue, holding hands, Vera on one side, Dmitri on the other, the two small boys in the middle. In silence, they took their jackets off and exposed the words that Vera had sewed on their T-shirts. They proclaimed their wish to emigrate and stated that they had been waiting for over five years.

I pretended to be a passer-by just a few yards away. Nearby, a foreign journalist was taking notes. A *militsioner*, a Soviet policeman, rushed up to the journalist and grabbed the pad from his hands. The fellow started to shout that he wanted his pad back, first in Russian, then in French. But to no avail. The *militsioner* took the pad, put it in his pocket, and walked away slowly, self-confident, looking around at the few pedestrians who, like me, were nearby.

A police van arrived soon afterwards. Several policemen in civilian clothes got out, handcuffed the family, and hustled them into the van. Vova, Vera 's youngest son, barely three years old, started to cry hysterically, berserk with fear. I placed my hands over my ears, I could not stand hearing him. The van sped away.

I drove home fast, I wanted to tell a few people what I had seen. Oksana was in the apartment as busy as ever. I told her about the family's demonstration that I, and other foreigners, had witnessed. Oksana listened in silence, keeping her shutters down. As I made calls a few minutes later, my phone went dead. I returned to Oksana and told her the strange coincidence. What kind of country was I living in? I asked her. Oksana assured me that the family would be released soon, the government would not be interested in jailing them since so many foreigners already knew about the incident.

Oksana did not hum a single tune that day. Just before she left, I remembered my request of the week: I had asked her to find a rope, preferably a thick one. I wanted a goodbye gift for a friend who was getting married in the south of France. Someone had organized a party with a theme: "It's fun to get married!" The guests were asked to bring presents that the groom was supposed to open with closed eyes.

Oksana had brought the rope, she took it out of her bag and handed it to me. But she said in a somber voice that a rope was not something to play with.

"I know Oksana," I said absent-mindedly. "But you are good with your hands, can you make a large noose at one end?" I looked at her. "This is for a friend who is getting married. He dated the bride only for a few months. With this gift, he can always hang himself if the marriage breaks up."

Oksana half-closed her shutters, it was clear that she disapproved of my idea. So I added quickly, as an excuse, "I guess only in this country would I have thought of such a souvenir." And I added, "I must have the plot of *Demons* on my mind."

Oksana had her shutters completely closed now but she was forming the noose I had requested. She did not need to look at her hands. And, suddenly, I had an uncanny feeling that Oksana had a reason to behave this way.

"Did you ever see someone hanged?" I asked as if struck by lightning.

"Da, *madame*, da," she answered.

"Where on earth, Oksana?"

Oksana opened her eyelids fully now. "In the Ukraine, during Second World War, my village was a battlefield; first there was infighting with the Germans, after that with the Russians. Bodies were left hanging in the main square to rot for days on end. Every villager, child and adult, saw them. I was young, we were all petrified." My own eyelids were wide open now.

"*Madame*, but those killings only followed Stalin's mass murders during the thirties."

I told Oksana to put the rope in the garbage, that I had had a silly idea.

Spring went by slowly. I often reflected how Oksana had been right: Vera and her family had been freed a few hours after their arrest; too many foreigners had been witnesses. Also, to my chagrin, I never bumped into Svetlana and Olga.

As usual, I left for Portugal during the summer. While I was away, Oksana told Keith with tears in her eyes that she could not work for us any more, that she was not allowed to. When I returned to Moscow I tried to find my pearl, dear

Oksana. She did not have a telephone at home, and I did not know her address. I asked the UPDK embassy employees repeatedly why Oksana was not working for us anymore. Finally the reply came, that Oksana had left the job at her own request.

As if that had been possible.

At the Levins'

Keith and I visited the Levins many times while we were in Moscow. Greg worked for a research institute and his wife, Xenia, stayed at home taking care of the two children, Natasha and Yuri. The family lived in a four-room cooperative apartment on the east side of the Moscow outer Ring Road. They had paid a fortune for the place, 7,000 rubles, and how they got the money I will never know. Greg's name had been passed on to Keith when a colleague left the American Embassy, for what reason I also will never know.

The apartment's floor space had been carefully arranged. The dining room was also the sitting room and the parents' bedroom. This way the children could each have their own separate space and Greg his office at home. That the building was an inhuman, massive structure, or that the floor layout was the same in adjacent buildings, did not bother them in the least. After sharing a communal apartment with others for many years, they thoroughly enjoyed the privacy that the new place provided.

The Levins were afraid to come to our apartment, so their lavish dinners went unreciprocated. Although still risky, it was safer for them to meet us in their own territory. As usual when going to Soviets' homes, we made all arrangements by word of mouth. The Levins requested that if we were followed, we not show up at their place. They also asked that we refrain from speaking English on the way up.

Lastly, they asked that if someone suspicious were to enter the elevator, we should elude them by pressing the button for a different floor.

The Levins were good people, and Keith and I felt at home in their place. Their *khlebosolstvo*, or hospitality, was, indeed, like the bread and the salt of the earth. Every time we visited, the children were inordinately gracious to us.

The four of them rushed to the entrance door one Sunday evening when we visited. They all knew Keith and I would be leaving the Soviet Union soon. Greetings started as soon as Greg shut the door.

"Welcome, welcome," he said. "Laura, let me help with your coat." Xenia added, "Here, Keith, give me your jacket, I'll hang it on the coat rack."

Keith and I presented the children with a couple of small gifts. "Natasha," I said, "I didn't forget to bring your beloved Swiss chocolates."

Natasha thanked me in English, her dark brown eyes filled with joy. I could see that she was wearing her best dress, pale yellow with white dots, immaculately clean and well ironed.

"And for you, Yuri," Keith said, addressing the seventeen-year-old boy, "I brought a book by Joyce, *Portrait of the Artist as a Young Man*. I think you'll enjoy it." Like his father, Yuri loved foreign books.

Our presence gave the children the opportunity to practice English. Natasha, ten years old, attended a prestigious Muscovite school where English was taught for several hours a day, the same school where Yuri had been a student earlier. Initially a bit shy, the children warmed up as the visit proceeded, but with Yuri always more reserved than Natasha.

Xenia welcomed us into the living area, where she, Natasha, and I started to talk on one side; the three men gathered across the room.

I enjoyed making small talk with the mother and daughter. Natasha was a bright girl, her British accent already pronounced. She was plump due to her mother's good cooking, and very well mannered. She delighted in showing me her English textbooks, industriously organized by height on her bedroom shelf.

"Natasha, can I see your English books?" I teased. "Last year your books were so well kept that I'm not sure you even opened them."

"Of course I did. How else would I study?" Natasha answered, her shyness showing in her red cheeks.

"Well, show me the new ones, then."

Natasha brought in a couple of books meticulously bound in dark brown wrapping paper and spread them on her parents' bed, where we were sitting. The bed was covered with a dark red bedspread, cheap cotton imitating damask.

"These books are also in very good shape. Let's see what you've learned."

"We're studying the geography and history of the British Isles now," Natasha answered in the manner of a grown-up. "Do you want me to recite? The texts are very long."

"No, don't recite. Use your own words."

Natasha paused, thinking. I saw her bewilderment, words escaped her. She opened her mouth, as if about to speak, but closed it again; she bit her lips.

"May I recite the first text?" she asked a second time.

"No, I prefer to hear your own words. You know English is also my second language, my native language is Portuguese. I know English can be strange and difficult," I said.

Natasha could not stand it any more. She started, reciting, "The United Kingdom, also known as Britain, is made up of England, Wales, Scotland, and Northern Ireland. London, the capital, has a population of ..."

Xenia looked proudly on, listening to her daughter in a

language she could hardly speak. She was in her middle forties, a graceful woman in a flowery, crepe de chine dress.

"Do you see, Laura," she interrupted, "how much Natasha has learned? You cannot imagine the hours she spent memorizing this."

"Yes, and her English is flawless, perfect."

"Truly?"

"Absolutely."

"Oh, I'm so happy! Maybe my daughter will marry a foreigner one day. Leave this country and have a better life."

Natasha was not happy to lose my attention. As soon as her mother stopped, she continued, "The fact that England is an island has protected her from major enemies. England is a Constitutional Monarchy, with a parliamentary system of government."

"How long is this text?" I asked as I turned the pages to see for myself.

"This one is at least ten pages, and she knows it all by heart," her mother beamed with satisfaction.

"Natasha, I see your English continues to improve. Your memory is also great. Just tell me now how the text ends."

Pleased, Natasha collected her thoughts. "Fine," she said, as I followed the lines in the textbook resting on my lap. "The British working-class has not yet freed itself from the capitalistic yoke, but she must, and she will—very soon."

Xenia and I listened to the last words and fell silent. We exchanged a glance, and I guessed Xenia did not approve of the last sentence. But I did not want to inquire, I did not feel it was right. For me, the ending of the text was provocative material to discuss. But I restrained myself, Natasha's face was too real, too good. I thanked her for the superb performance and let her go.

My eyes turned now to the girl's framed picture over the counter near the opposite wall: Natasha with a big, trusting smile, the red scarf of the Pioneers, the children's communist organization, around her neck. I noticed that the picture had been printed by Kodak, the American company must have had a subsidiary in Moscow. Xenia explained that they always came to take the children's photos at the beginning of the school year.

Xenia went to the kitchen and soon announced that lunch was ready. The six of us sat at the table to eat. As in a Russian feast, the table was fully covered with delicacies. Our hostess presented the usual *zakuski*, cucumber, beet, and mushroom salads, and various dips to accompany them; along with *pelmeni*, Siberian dumplings, and a tureen of vegetable soup. One large tray displayed pieces of pickled herring and another tray slices of pork accompanied by mashed potatoes. The various loaves of white and dark bread were a reminder, if need be, of how the Levins honored their guests.

As Xenia filled our plates the conversation between the adults became animated. The children kept to themselves, eating.

"This country isn't improving, not even with Gorbachev in power now. We're happy Chernenko died so soon after replacing Andropov, but this is not enough. The young want new things and we can't get them," Greg said.

"What are you referring to?" Keith asked.

"Everything. Take the example of blue jeans. Every American has, at least, one pair, maybe two or three. We can't find them here." I looked at Yuri. He was dressed very much like his father in a clean, well-ironed checkered shirt and a pair of dark brown pants.

"We don't agree with the new consumer culture, *veshch-izm*, we don't think that people need to have all they want. But with certain items life is much easier," Greg said between forkfuls.

"The time spent trying to find what we need is unreal," Xenia added, looking at me. "If a housewife needs something in America, she goes to the store and buys it. Here it takes weeks of searching."

Xenia continued to fill the plates as we talked. I slowed down, the only way to prevent her from putting more food on my plate. With the vodka and the wine it was even more difficult, as Greg kept pouring them without asking if I wanted more.

"Let's make a toast," Greg said, after refilling the glasses with vodka, "To Russia, without the Soviet Union." The adults toasted, but I noticed that Yuri did not raise his eyes from his plate.

"At least, to better conditions in this country," Keith replied as he looked at Yuri. We all drank to that, too.

Greg was interested in salaries in America, how much one must earn to be able to travel abroad, prices of various foods, apartments, cars. Keith gave him answers as precise as the questions. Between eating and talking, the meal went on forever.

When we finished, Xenia got up and went to the kitchen. Natasha disappeared into her room and returned wearing a simpler dress to help her mother clean up. I removed a few plates but returned to sit with the men at the table. Xenia brought Turkish coffee in demitasse cups.

Greg, Yuri, and Keith were now discussing Yuri's current difficulties. "Last June I took the university's entrance examinations and passed two of them," Yuri said. "But I felt the professor wanted me to fail on the last one."

"Why?" Keith asked.

"We're Jewish, that's why. My ethnic origins are written in my passport. I'm sure he knew about it." Yuri paused. "But I'm already studying hard again for the exams next year. I hope I'll pass."

Xenia brought some homemade éclairs, and we all bit into them.

"Yuri has always been a very good student. This was a

big blow," Greg said with sadness stamped on his face.

"What exam did you fail?" Keith asked again.

"Party affiliation, party loyalty, Marxism-Leninism. We need to know all that."

"Did your friends pass?"

"Some did," Yuri replied.

"Take Gennadi, the son of a well-known journalist, he got into the school of journalism," Greg added, unhappily. "I'm sure his father taught him to recite all the garbage."

"How unfair it all seems," I burst out.

"People here are ruthless, they'll do anything to keep their privileges," Greg threw in, breathless.

"Why do you think being Jewish affected you?" Keith asked Yuri.

"They don't want us in positions of power, they like to keep us down," Greg was the one to reply.

"You don't think Gorbachev will be able to change that?" Keith asked of Greg.

"*Perestroika*, the restructuring that Gorbachev wants to implement, might take quite some time. Our system is very rigid, opening it might not be so easy," Greg answered.

Yuri interjected, "I already gave up journalism, it's too much in the front line. But I want to do history," he continued assertively. "Like my friends, I want a good life. I want to work on something I like, to buy things, to be able to travel. This is why I need to enter the university. A technical institute will not do."

"Why not?" Keith asked again.

"If I attend a technical school," Yuri answered, "I'll have a low salary for the rest of my life."

"This system seems so undemocratic," I scoffed.

I noticed a change in Yuri when I said that. He looked at me and said quite seriously, "This country is a democracy. The constitution was written by more than one thousand people." Yuri might have failed his exam but he knew the

Marxist-Leninist jargon.

Greg answered, "Son, in a true democracy people are free to say what they think. The people chosen to write the constitution were party people, loyal to the system."

Yuri replied as if thinking aloud, "But here people work for their own good, for the country's development, to build socialism. They don't give the profits of their work to their bosses." He looked his father in the eyes and added, "The dictatorship of the proletariat is real in this country."

While Yuri recited the lesson that he had learned in school, Greg picked up his fork and played with bits and pieces of an éclair.

Now the silence filled the room and I thought about the strong Stalinist legacy, the fears families still had. Parents were afraid of their children reporting them to the state, children were afraid their parents might do the same. People became traitors in their own homes, accusing their own flesh and blood; relatives turned against their own kind.

I felt outraged. "Yuri, I want you to visit the *gastronom* on the ground floor of the building where we live in Bolshaya Ordynka Street. Look at the men unloading the meat in that shop. Look at that working class, look at their faces. Then tell me how liberated they appear to you."

As I spoke I remembered the prematurely aged, perpetually half-drunk men that I had seen so many times through my window. These men—dressed in white overcoats stained with sticky, old blood — bent forward under the weight of carcasses, their heads close to the floor.

Yuri stared at me, and his eyes turned dark with rage. "What's wrong with those faces? In socialism everybody works."

"I don't know if everybody works in socialism. Productivity is quite low in this country." I continued, "And from what I see, not everybody looks the same, the higher-ups look much better. I see them everywhere: in their boxes at the Bolshoi Theater, at embassy receptions, in the *beryozki*. These are party people, not proletariats; they live very well and have unique privileges. The *beryozki* are special stores, the poor aren't allowed inside."

Keith and Greg exchanged a quick glance, the lines around Greg's mouth looked deeper. Yuri did not reply, but I could see he was upset. Instead of keeping quiet, as I had when Natasha mentioned the "capitalist yoke," this time I had been unable to restrain myself.

Keith looked at me with cold, distant eyes, but, forever the diplomat, he addressed Greg, "Well, at least Yuri is learning his lesson. He shouldn't have any trouble passing the exams next time."

Xenia and Natasha were resting on the sofa that doubled as a bed. Natasha was falling asleep sitting next to her mother, her head leaning against the cozy bosom. While we talked at the table, Xenia had already yawned twice. Mother and daughter must have gotten up quite early to prepare the delicious meal.

Keith got up from the table and turned to me saying, "Laura, we've talked too much already, I think it's time to go." Usually, to leave might take as long as half an hour. This time, not knowing if we would see the family again, we needed time for good-byes and good wishes.

As we headed to the door, I wanted to make up with Yuri. Without intending to, I had hurt him during what might have been our last visit. As Greg helped me with my coat, I addressed the young man. "I'm terribly sorry if I upset you, Yuri. I really didn't mean to."

Yuri only shrugged his shoulders, but I wanted Yuri back as a friend. "I understand that you want to go to a university and make a good living in this country. I realize that you need to compromise."

Yuri lowered his eyes, a grimace on his face. I continued like a crusader, "But I hope you'll use your mind creatively one day. As you look around, keep your feet on the ground."

Yuri, the vigor of youth stamped on his face, raised his eyes and asked defiantly of me, "Why? Why is it that I should use my mind creatively?"

A reply did not occur to me as quickly as I wished, I thought that the answer was self-evident from our conversation. As I searched for the *mot juste*, Keith replied, "Do you want to know why, Yuri? Do you really want an answer?"

"Yes, I do," Yuri said, still defiant.

"So here it goes," Keith turned his head slightly to the side, a habit of his for emotional effect. "It's because so very few people do it, some foreigners in this country included. That's why!"

Yuri did not reply but he smiled broadly. Clearly, Keith was referring to me.

We proceeded to embrace affectionately. Natasha put her arms around me. Xenia gave me a couple of chocolate éclairs to take home. The men exchanged handshakes and kisses, in threes, the Russian custom.

Greg opened and shut the apartment door quickly. Keith pushed the elevator's button, and we left the building in our usual hasty manner. As we approached our car, the wind running through the outer Ring Road did not bring the usual, expected feeling of lightness. Certainly not that day, certainly not that evening.

New Year's Eve at the Praga

It was my idea to spend New Year's Eve at the exclusive Praga restaurant. The year before, I did not think the hundreds of vodka bottles smashed in Red Square by the *narod*, the Russian people, were an omen of good luck. The combination of broken glass, ice, and snow seemed a chilling presage. This year I needed something warmer, closer to my heart. I craved a magical moment that could, unexpectedly, turn the New Year into something meaningful. I wished for a renewed feeling that life could, and should, be enjoyed to the fullest.

I called two friends to make arrangements to celebrate together—I chose Denise and Rose—and we ended up with a group of six people. I had consulted Keith previously, and he agreed to go out that evening; in fact, it was our last New Year's celebration in the Soviet Union. Denise and Rose knew each other fairly well as both had been my confidantes during our stay in the country. Their husbands, Tony Edmunds and Brian Lewis, worked with Keith in the embassy's upper floors.

I chose the Praga, but not because I loved it; I always felt there as if in the middle of a third-class railroad restaurant in the Western World. Since the place seated more than fifteen hundred people at a time, the atmosphere was neither charming nor cozy. Table after table filled the gigantic dining rooms, therefore the space lacked a sense of intimacy. Food and service also left much to be desired. But people had told me that the Russian clientele really enjoyed this Soviet holiday, and that the Praga's New Year's celebration was usually festive.

The restaurant was famous in Moscow, it was a large, pre-revolutionary, three-story yellow building. And it was located in a prominent area, the Arbat. I enjoyed Okudzhava's romantic song about the neighborhood, "Oh, Arbat, my Arbat..." As far as I was concerned, the song had aged better than the place itself—but the massive reconstruction going on could be responsible for this impression.

Anticipating a full house our group arrived promptly at ten o'clock. We were all looking quite elegant. Keith chose a more casual look than most of us and wore a dark-gray, silk turtleneck. Denise, Rose, and I had squandered hours on the phone deciding what to wear. Amongst the men, Tony looked undoubtedly the best—he wore a bright blue velvet Italian bow tie and reminded me, somehow, of a splendid Persian horse.

The Russians were all stunningly attired. As we entered the cloakroom, countless finely shaped fur coats—astrakhan, mink, fox—paraded by. The *narod* had, indeed, been excluded from the Praga's closed doors. Excitement shone in people's faces, eyes, manner. Some men wore tuxedos, bow ties in perfect place. The women were dressed in attractive, black dresses. They glowed with carefully applied make-up, their hair stylishly arranged at the beauty parlor only hours before. A frivolous mood filled the air.

I noticed a young blond woman as we came in, her hairstyle at first. The long golden hair fell down straight, parted to one side and sophisticatedly brought together by a large hairpin. The pin, in the shape of a butterfly, was exactly the same color as her hair. Her skin had the mark of leisure, and revealed a veneer of gracefully applied make-up. The freshness of good care was obvious, the work of many hours spent at the sauna to clean every possible pore.

As I looked on, her companion placed her fur coat on his arm and waited in line to give it to the attendant. He was also young and, in contrast to her, rather ordinary. She examined the entrance room and found a chair while waiting for him. Seated, she looked a bit *ennuyée* but, unlike most Russian women, she crossed her legs placing them at the perfect angle.

As my friends and I entered the ancient elevator to reach the Winter Garden Room on the top floor—where our table had been reserved—I addressed Keith in a low voice, "I hope your turtleneck measures up to the occasion. I know you wanted to feel comfortable, but I wish you had put on a dark suit like Tony and Brian."

"The way I look doesn't make any difference."

"It makes a difference to me, it has to do with looking your best for a New Year's party. Look at the Russians—my God!—they all look superb. And look at me, I'm all dressed up. We are so mismatched."

Keith cracked a joke, "The moment is just mimicking our real life. Try not to worry. We want to have a good time, remember?"

I smiled and turned my attention to the extra care placed in the decoration and cleanliness of the long corridors we were passing through. The red and cream carpet was old, its geometrical design long faded with pieces of old wool hanging loosely from the sides. But the floor did not look as greasy as in the past; it had been recently polished. The chandeliers were not missing a single light bulb, and the usual spider webs did not dangle down loosely. Flowers, expensive as they were during the winter, adorned many of the sideboards.

We finally found the Winter Garden Room and looked for our table. It was round, well placed, not too close to the band. Tony looked so handsome that I made sure I sat between him and Keith. Rose was to Keith's left since she always enjoyed his intellectual conversation. Brian sat next to Rose, and Denise between Tony and Brian. All seemed pleased with the seating arrangements.

The Winter Garden was getting more packed and noisy by the minute. At its center stood a large marble fountain filled with water, its columns decorated with multiple garlands of silver and gray tinsel. The tinsel's two shades of color superbly matched the somber-looking marble. Our table, like the others, had a wide variety of *zakuski*: boiled eggs stuffed with mayonnaise and the best of black and red caviar, a wide variety of the famous Russian breads, and an assortment of fresh salads, including cabbage, beet, cucumber, tomatoes, and olives. There were several bottles of carbonated water, a favorite Russian refreshment; and Georgian and Moldavian white and red wines, already opened.

The atmosphere warmed up gradually towards midnight, when the action really started. Ten minutes before the magical moment, an army of waiters entered the room to fill our glasses with champagne. Bottles popped, fizzed, and gushed. Tony, always protecting his bow tie with his hand to make sure the waiters did not spill on it, kept calling the waiters over to our table. Five minutes later, loudspeakers announced New Year's greetings from the Central Committee of the Communist Party, as reported on radio and television. At the stroke of midnight everyone rose to sing the Soviet national anthem. When they finished, I suggested that we sing "America, the Beautiful." But Keith, the ultimate diplomat, thought "Silent Night" was more appropriate, and this is what we sang. The Russians stood up, listening. Minutes later Ded Moroz, or Grandfather Frost, and Snegurochka, the small Snow Maiden, made a grand entrance distributing sweet cookies.

The Russians became loud and expansive as the ambiance turned more and more extravagant. Vodka toasts abounded lavishly around us, "Long live the peoples of the Soviet Republics!"

"To the good health of my dear, beloved, friend Nikolay Aleksandrovich!"

"To peace and friendship around the world!"

"To all the women in the room and particularly to the women at this table!"

Feeling demonstrative, I rose from my seat and grabbed Keith from behind his shoulders. I brought my champagne near his mouth and tried to make him drink from my glass. I toasted in English, "To our departure from this wretched country, to warmer climates, and more congenial lands."

Using an official sounding tone of voice, Keith replied without drinking from my glass, "Speak for yourself, Laura. Everybody is having a good time here."

"Here, the Praga, or here, the country?" I asked, baffled. Keith did not respond to my request to drink from my glass, and now he was challenging me.

"Both, as a matter of fact."

"You and the duplicity of your words!" I replied, angered.

But the band interrupted our conversation with its exceptionally loud noise. To suit the happy occasion it started playing several patriotic Russian tunes. Perhaps Keith did not like my comment about the wretched country; the Soviets around us might have understood my English. I found the general mood too jolly to agonize over what I had said. The band played on, still incredibly noisy, and people sang along at the top of their lungs. After a while the band turned to Italian music from the sixties, which sounded very old-fashioned. Several male singers lurched back and forth in their weary, sluggish styles, an invitation for everyone to take to the dance floor. Tony and Denise were the first among us to dance. After a while the space became so crowded that people were swing-dancing in between the tables.

As I looked onto the dance floor I noticed the young blonde dancing with her drab friend near the band. They accompanied the tune facing each other but not in sync. She was definitely stealing the show. Each of her movements required thought and care as she moved herself lavishly in front of his eyes. But her facial expression and closed eyes showed that she was not dancing with or for her partner. She was only dancing for herself—or maybe for the audience.

She wore a skin-tight, black mini-skirt exquisitely draped in two layers and a skimpy lamé top with no bra. Her breasts were small and round, two firm peaches softly moving with the beat. Her tights were also black, and she had on shiny shoes. She accompanied each song with her lips as if kissing someone. Men could not take their eyes off her. I looked at Keith, but he was talking to Rose, he did not seem to have noticed the blonde.

Soon afterwards I asked Keith to dance with me and he agreed. Next to us a middle-aged couple swung about in full embrace, looking into each other's eyes, as if by themselves. He was bald; she was fat, stout. Once in a while the man whispered something to her; she smiled adoringly. I admired their emotional rapport, their closeness. And I asked myself if the love that this woman visibly enjoyed was the result of her ability to share her life, the good and the bad. Or rather, I continued to myself, was this love a present, a possible gift from the gods.

Holding on to his neck and pointing to the couple, I asked Keith, "Have you seen those two dancing? The world seems theirs, they are having such a good time."

"Yes, they are."

"I wish we could be the same."

"So do I, but you act insatiable."

"What do you mean?"

"It's your attitude. You squeeze the blood out of me. You

need to back off if you want me closer."

"You confuse me. It seems you see my wishing to feel intimate with you as a weakness."

"No, of course I don't. But you're too demanding—of me, my time, even my work." Keith continued, "I'm trying to build my foreign-service career starting from this country, a rival country to my own. But as much as the Soviets, sometimes you act like an adversary."

"I left my entire life to be here with you. I went through too many changes too fast." I tried to be precise with my words, "I live in a no-man's land. And some of our experiences have been rather painful, grant me that."

"I try to, but sometimes it takes a toll on me."

"I find your job too absorbing, I get jealous of it."

Keith did not answer but held me eagerly, it made me feel good. We danced to two or three more songs tightly embraced. When we sat again, we exchanged a warm smile, one that only accomplices might share.

Our friends were having a great time at the table. They were exchanging New Year's greetings in various Eastern European languages; also, vodka for champagne with the Soviet people at the nearest table. When the loudspeakers announced that our table had won the room's cake lottery—and the hotel manager on duty that evening delivered it in person—Denise brought our neighbors a large piece. Then, engaging Tony as well, she moved her chair aside and talked with the ladies sitting behind. Brian, blissful, sipped his wine. Rose, with impeccable manners, invited someone from that table to dance with her. Already holding the man's hand, she urged me to pick someone else.

But I did not want to. I decided to watch our neighbors' most opulent lady as she took to the dance floor by herself. She weighed well over two hundred pounds and her dancing seemed a rare tribute to the Soviet brassiere. These women seem the center of the universe, I thought to myself, men only gravitate around them. My eyes paused on the blonde again. She had eased to the edge of the dance floor. Moving herself with her studied rhythm, she had her eyes half-open now and seemed to be looking at a distant horizon. I pictured her dreaming of foreign lands. Her lips continued with the kissing game, as if unable to stop or slow down. Her partner seemed oblivious to the attention converging upon her.

Men watched, hanging from her every move. I turned my eyes toward Keith again. He was discussing a recent piece of international news with Brian. When our eyes met, he returned my glance, I was not sure where he had been looking before.

Dinner was served rather late in the evening. The *zakuski* were long gone, and we were all starving. As Brian plunged his teeth into a goose leg accompanied by sweet apples, he asked with a sparkle in his eye, "Where is that blonde? I haven't seen her in a while." And, turning to Tony, "What do you think, shall we invite her to have some cake with us?"

"Why not? I would enjoy her company," Tony replied, evidently amused.

Denise turned to him, a grimace on her face, "Oh, you would, would you?"

"She seems fun, and she's so skinny she might profit from some cake."

"Tony, you're incorrigible," Denise looked at him lovingly, entertained.

Brian smiled at Denise, "Tony is absolutely right. And that blonde, whoever she is, good or bad, has certainly contributed to the civilized atmosphere this evening," he said, an ironic tone to his voice.

Rose stared at her husband straight in the eyes and said, "Stop deluding yourself. You know you want to dance with her, Brian. Asking her to share our cake will only tease you."

Brian did not answer, but he looked at the empty dance floor again. I glanced at Keith. He had raised his eyes when Brian mentioned the blonde, but, again, I was not sure if he was searching the room for her.

Coffee and plombir, a delicate ice cream, finished the meal. Our appetites satisfied, we got very silly. Denise went to the fountain in the middle of the room and took a few pieces of tinsel that she wove into her curls. Then she brought some for us to decorate ourselves as well. Rose placed a thin garland around her décolleté. I fancied myself a princess, a silver tiara around my head. Brian, as silly as I ever saw him, strung the tinsel from ear to ear. Tony touched his bow tie and decided that it sufficed.

Keith's eyes sparkled at me, and he said that for a princess only a prince would do. He made a crown mixing gray and silver tinsel and embellished his head with it. His silk turtleneck had become a royal armor.

Following Brian's eyes, I looked at the dance floor and realized that the blonde had returned. She was rather close to our table now, barely four or five feet away. I could smell a new fragrance in the air, sort of sweet sour, not exactly delicate but certainly sensuous. Instead of the semi-closed eyes of before, they were fully opened now. And she was trying to make eye contact with the men at our table. As she observed them, I noticed the almost indistinguishable motion of her eyes. She seemed undecided, she still did not have any one in mind. She studied Tony's velvet bow tie; Brian, blond like her, in his dark blue suit with tinsel from ear to ear; and Keith, a Prince Charming at the moment.

Rose, hoping to distract the men, invited everybody to play the wishing game. A token charm for the New Year, she announced. She laid out the rules. No one could decline to play and everyone had to write down an anonymous wish on a piece of paper and fold it tight. As I passed around a porcelain tray decorated with tiny tangerines, everyone placed his or her wish in the middle. Among roars of laughter and noise, Denise told me to read them aloud. I opened the pieces of paper slowly, enjoying the attention, thoughtfully reading the different handwritings. To my surprise, I realized that I could not recognize Keith's lettering on any of the pieces of paper. Someone wanted twins, another a gold tooth as a lucky charm, someone else a new assignment to the Pacific Islands. A woman's handwriting wished for a house in the American suburbs, a swimming pool and a tennis court included; another wished for Tony's bow tie. Using printing to make sure he remained unidentified, someone ventured a new appetite: to have the blonde to himself at the Ritz Hotel in Madrid.

Everyone felt free to dream, if only for a night. But who wanted the blond woman, I wondered? Was it Keith? I really could not tell.

We left at dawn, the dim morning light already shining through the windows. As we put our coats on to leave the Praga, there was the blonde again. Her escort was nowhere to be seen. The young woman now wore a long shawl that barely covered her slender shoulders. It was an exquisite piece of silk with colorful wildflower seeds in featherlike shapes, their names embroidered in Cyrillic. She seemed ready for anything—her own New Year's wishes only a step away.

"We had a great time!" exclaimed Keith turning to me with his eyes barely open.

"We really did," I answered, thrilled.

"You know what? The Soviets are forever offering us money in exchange for the western clothing we wear. It's my turn to be daring. I'm going to offer the blonde 100 rubles for that shawl."

"Great idea! Let's throw it on our bed tonight," I said feeling as wild as the flower seeds themselves. "Everybody's talking about *glasnost* these days. We can start with ourselves, by opening our hearts to each other."

Keith headed toward the blonde. "I promise you," he called back to me," this will be our best New Year's ever."